I0533780

A Boo or Two for You

Luke Swanson

Published by Luke Swanson, 2025.

This is a work of fiction. Similarities to real people, places, or events are entirely coincidental.

A BOO OR TWO FOR YOU

First edition. September 30, 2025.

Copyright © 2025 Luke Swanson.

ISBN: 979-8999737212

Written by Luke Swanson.

Table of Contents

The Six-Foot Ladder

Freaky Factor: 2/3

A FEW THINGS ABOUT me:

My name is Ramona Price. I was born in October 1934, which means I'm currently 21 years old. For the past several years, I've been on the run. My nerves are always on edge, and I've learned to sleep less than five hours a night.

Why?

Because I've always seen the specters.

For as long as I can remember, they've walked alongside me, staring straight ahead. Paying me no mind. They talk to one another, laugh, nod, cry, and basically go about their lives. Or their unlives, I suppose. Sometimes they disappear, or soar through the air like wraiths, or contort into horrifying shapes.

But they never look at me. That's almost worse than it would be if they targeted me or something like that. I know that sounds ridiculous—why would I *want* to be haunted by ghosts?

When their crystal eyes pass right over me, though, it's as if they don't even want to waste their endless time on me.

That's worse. A great deal worse.

I sit in the driver's seat of my Ford Coupe, barreling through Podunk-Nowhere, Oklahoma. There's nothing but horizon, the occasional spindly tree, and the asphalt ribbon stretching on and on and on in front of me. "Rock Around the Clock" by Bill Haley is stuck in my head, which I'm grateful for, because there's absolutely no scenery to keep me occupied. I've already hummed through all of

"Singin' in the Rain" twice. At least, all of "Singin' in the Rain" that I can remember.

The ripe orange sun in the center of the pale sky makes everything shimmer and flicker, like images on a projected screen. The heat is almost unbearable, and the open windows only succeed in mussing my hair and letting in uninvited mosquitos. I've heard that a lot of the brand-new Chryslers and Cadillacs now come with systems that regulate the temperature inside your car, so that you could shiver in July or wear a sundress on Christmas. On the opposite side of the spectrum, my dirt-brown '35 Ford needs a kick and a prayer to get started, and it looks like it's winking when I drive at night.

It's a cruddy car, to be sure, but in this new place, I'll need something I'm familiar with in order to not spiral into insanity.

I glance into the backseat to take a quick inventory:

Six dresses on wire hangers. My old high-pop automatic toaster, charred crumbs still trapped in its belly. A few pairs of brown house shoes and my red heels in case I need to gussy up. And a mid-sized suitcase, its hinges and latches straining from its contents.

Yep. Everything I own in the world, in my backseat. Not exactly a pharaoh's treasure trove, but it's gotten me this far.

Why?

I shake my head to dislodge that nagging question, but it remains all the same.

Why did I leave the city?

The worst part is, I know the answer. I know without a doubt that I needed to leave Oklahoma City. The specters make it easy to not look back. The streets are haunted for me, the tall buildings more like valkyries than sentinels. The city used to be so full of promise, bustling and energetic, thrumming with the rhythm of thousands of souls, thousands of heartbeats. I could stroll down any given road and see joy embodied in the people. Businessmen, young mothers, nomadic artists, dogs on leashes... OKC was a fascinating amalgamation of mega metropolis and cozy Main Street, a sprawling city with the tenderness of a small town.

Was.

It had been like a lightswitch. On one second, off the next. As warm as OKC had been, it suddenly became twice as arctic. I'd never felt so alone, despite being surrounded by people. The population began to reject me like a failed kidney transplant. I would walk along West Main in a desperate attempt to recapture my previous sense of contentment. But nothing. The businessmen jostled past me, the young mothers scoffed and turned their heads away. The dogs even bared their crusty teeth.

And the specters sure didn't help. They usually avoid crowded areas, preferring to show up when I'm alone. But the coldness of the city seemed to draw them out. Ghostly figures staggered among the population. Huge, toothy grins stretched across their faces, cackling like madmen. Or aggressive, poisonous eyes, itching to attack. Or blank stares, as if lost in a supermarket. And still, they never looked directly at me.

I couldn't take it anymore. In addition to the hostility of the living, the terror of the dead sealed the deal.

So when the winds turned from pleasant to dusty and wet laundry dried almost instantly on the line, I decided it was time to leave. I stripped my apartment bare, loaded all my worldly possessions in the back of my Ford, and left.

I had no destination, no plan. I just needed to leave.

So here I am, bulleting through the empty plains of dusty Oklahoma. Nothingness stretches in every direction, flat as a pancake—I'm almost impressed. It's like some sort of purgatory from a Kafka novel.

I smirk to myself. At least the college degree stuffed in my suitcase is good for something, if only making obscure literary references in my head.

Then I see one. A strange man in a strange suit, standing in the middle of the road. A specter. The very thing I'm running from.

I freeze, but my Ford continues to scream onward. Directly toward the specter, like a locomotive careening along its fixed tracks.

And yet, time seems to slow. I get a good look at the man, this earth-bound shadow shackled to my world like a prisoner of war.

I'm a hundred yards from him and closing fast.

He's tall and lanky like Jack's beanstalk, but with wide shoulders that could knock down a locked door—that is, if he needed to use a door. Dark hair stands up straight from his scalp as if trying to escape. His eyes are wide and round, vibrating in his skull. He staggers across my path, jerkily stomping one foot in front of the other, like a demented version of a "chicken crossing the road" joke. His clothing is strange, as if from another country that isn't to be founded for another century—familiar enough, but also completely alien. I can even see his clenched jaw, balled fists, and bumpy gray skin.

I'm fifty yards away.

Without a doubt, he's a wraith, a reaper, a phantom. But he also looks like a man, and that's what thrashes my nerves.

Twenty yards.

He doesn't glance at me, even as my automobile speeds directly toward him. I'm nothing to him. And *that's* what turns my blood to ice.

Ten.

I clench my eyes shut and brace for impact.

But, of course, I don't feel anything. My Ford just keeps cruising along. I pry my eyes open and see the ribbon of road, the horizon, the dusty Okie landscape, and the ripe orange sun.

Yep, I've passed right through him. As I always do. But I can never help it—I always think I'll hit them, hurt them, kill them. But they don't even mind me running over them.

My hands would be trembling if I weren't grasping the steering wheel so tightly. This is a strategic move. But the white knuckles and bulging tendons start to unsettle me, so I force my muscles to relax.

This isn't easy to do. I'm a bit like a jack-in-the-box—tightly wound within my own confines, always waiting to pop, wearing garish clothes, and probably ruining someone's day.

That's not all true. I think I dress pretty well.

I shake my head to clear the wandering thoughts. The road before me demands my attention.

Even so, I glance in the rearview mirror.

The specter is gone.

Their existence is still a mystery to me. I've lived among these misty, grotesque apparitions for as long as my memory can reach, yet I don't know their purpose. Who are they? Why are they so disfigured? Where do they come from? Where are they headed? Why am I the only person plagued by their presence?

I have no answers. The specters—the phantasms that define my very life, temperament, and reality—are one gigantic question mark.

It drives me crazy. Hence my less-than-five-hours-of-sleep-a-night habit.

I see a road sign up ahead: a squat, blue rectangle emblazoned with three words.

"*Welcome to Crawford.*"

A town this far out in the middle of limbo? I squint. Sure enough, in the distance, I spot silhouettes of buildings, structures, and even a few trees.

Should I pull over here, call Crawford my new oasis? I've never even heard of this town. My foot rests a little heavier upon my Ford's accelerator. Maybe the next city...

The residual memory of the specter practically slaps me. His wild eyes, the ramrod-straight hair.

I switch my foot to the brake and decide to give Crawford a try.

Why not?

The air glistens as I pull my car onto the road leading to this unknown township. Deep creaking sounds rumble from beneath the Ford's hood, causing the entire car to tremble around me. I groan. After years of being faithful, it picks this moment to croak? Of course.

I caress the dashboard as if it's a nervous pet and whisper, "C'mon, old lady. Just a little bit further." As if that'll help. Hey, it's only a superstition if it doesn't work.

But the rumbling actually gets worse. I grit my teeth and will my Ford to keep going, but it's shaking like a newborn foal using its twiggy legs for the very first time. It's sure to buckle entirely any second.

"Go, old lady, I believe in you!"

Sputter.

"Don't do this to me..."

It does it to me. The engine goes quiet, the car's momentum continues for about forty yards...and I roll to a stop in the middle of the road.

The sun beats down mercilessly upon me, forming a layer of sweat on my skin. I rub my temples with my palms, forcing myself to focus, to block out the ridiculous heat, the specters that are sure to be lurking nearby, and the fact that my car has died on the outskirts of an unfamiliar town.

My situation just keeps getting better and better.

I punch the dashboard and growl, furious, wary, scared, lonely, tense... I'm drowning within my own mind.

I sit in the front seat for a moment, but it stretches into an eternity. I pull my breath in and push it out very slowly, decelerating my heart rate bit by bit. Gradually, I regain control.

You will not win.

I banish the specters from my mind. I refuse to let them burden me.

Before the dismal thoughts can sink their hooks back in, I kick open the car door and clamber out into the sandpaper air. Not only is it sizzling, but the Oklahoma wind slams into me like a pro linebacker, hopelessly mussing my hair and—even worse—whipping my dress up over my face. Now I'm blindfolded by a floral pattern, and my bloomers are exposed before God. I quickly shove my dress down into its proper position and hold it there against the deviant gusts. There may not be anyone around to see, but I still consider myself a proper lady.

Plus, I don't want to put on a peep show for any specters who might be passing by. We haven't quite reached that level yet.

The town of Crawford lurks about a mile away, flickering and waving at me through the heated air. Oklahoma City may not be New York or Los Angeles, but it's practically the golden age of Rome compared to the itty-bitty collection of buildings that calls itself a municipality. There can't be more than 500 people in the whole township, and that's a very generous estimate.

But I'm here in the first place because I'm leaving the big city behind, and my Ford Coupe isn't going anywhere without some motivation.

Looks like Crawford, Oklahoma, is the place to be.

I throw a glance at my bulging suitcase in the car. The dresses, the heels... It can all sit tight until I hire a mechanic to fix my old dirt-brown Coupe. I get the feeling it's safer out in the middle of this Midwestern desert than locked in a Swiss bank vault.

So I fix my gaze on the distant shadow of Crawford, crack my stiff neck joints, and get moving. As I walk, I make sure to ignore the misshapen, grunting specter to my left, just as it ignores me.

• • • •

THIS TOWN IS A SNOWGLOBE. Small, contained, daintily designed, and ornately painted, as picturesque as a postcard from heaven.

But small can be stifling. Contained can be restrictive. Dainty and ornate can be fragile and weak, and picturesque is often a mere façade disguising a hollow husk—a withering cocoon that once held a butterfly. One quick shake can send everything into chaos.

This is Crawford, Oklahoma. I tiptoe down the sidewalk, afraid to place my full weight on my soles lest I awaken a slumbering beast. I pass a street sign signaling that I'm walking along Main Street, which appears to spear the entire town, running from end to end. There's a boutique advertising both manicures and shaves, a squat bank building that seems to frown, a handful of wrought-iron streetlamps pulled from the pages of a Dickens tale, and a huge brick monstrosity branded the "Hughes County Mortuary"—with a cardboard sign in the window reading "You bag 'em, we tag 'em" in very polished calligraphy.

But not a sound.

No birds or footsteps or revving car engines or rattling bicycles.

No one is in sight. Not a soul. No mothers with children, no businessmen hustling to and fro, no families with faithful canines.

The entire town stands perfectly still, like a bronze monument to some past tragedy. Like a dollhouse waiting for its god to manipulate it.

A snowglobe, idyllic and ersatz all at once.

Suddenly, darkness covers the entire street, making the hairs on my arms stand at attention. I pause in front of the mortuary and look up. A dense cloud has swallowed the orange sun, blocking its heat and engulfing all of Crawford in an ethereal embrace.

I clench my fists against the chill. This town...

Something's wrong. My eyes dart across the buildings that line Main Street. Even besides the lack of people, there's an atmosphere about this place that makes my bones tingle. Something...off. Like department store mannequins that look only halfway lifelike. I can't quite put my finger on it—

Then it hits me.

There aren't any specters here.

None. At any given time, I usually see at least a handful. But there are none here.

Even they seem to know this place is wrong.

Click clap click clap.

My heart leaps.

Footsteps. A person!

I'd never dreamed that the sound of someone's loafers thumping against asphalt would be so glorious.

A man turns the corner onto Main. His watch is an inch from his pinched face, and his frenzied gait is that of a king late to his own coronation. His black suit is neat and pressed, including a snazzy waistcoat.

He isn't exactly the picture of a savior, but in the middle of this void, I couldn't be happier to see him. His cheeks are rosy and his eyes flash like azure lighthouses—he seems nice enough. I call out, "Mister! Hello?"

He slows for a moment, ear cocked curiously, but continues on his speedy way.

I huff. After my automotive woes, the trek on foot into town, and my encounter with the wide-eyed specter on the road, I'm more than a little frustrated. Digging for my most authoritative voice, I yell, "Hey!"

That stops him in his tracks. His shoulders clench and he looks around, searching for the source of the greeting. I take a few steps toward him, raising my hand for easy identification—although it can't be too hard to spot me in the middle of this empty, life-size toy set of a town. Then, his eyes land on me.

The rouge drains from his face immediately. He opens his mouth to speak, but only a gasp escapes.

"Umm...sir?" I walk toward him.

But he raises his arms toward me and shrieks, "No!" He staggers backward as if I have the Plague, tripping over his own feet in haste. "Stay away!" he hisses. "Go! Go!"

He pivots 180 degrees and sprints out of sight.

Click clap click clap click clap click clap.

Deafening silence smothers Main Street, and I stand frozen in front of the mortuary. My feet are bolted to the sidewalk—which is a very good thing, because I think I might topple over otherwise.

I don't understand. Why was that man so *afraid* of me?

Or...

He'd told me to go. To stay away. Could it be that he's afraid of this *town*?

My knees tremble under the weight of confusion. Or is it fear? Both? I can't even pinpoint my own frame of mind. All I feel for certain is the cold sweat on my brow and the bile in my throat.

"Good afternoon."

I yelp and spin toward the new voice. Leaning against the doorframe of the mortuary's entrance is a long-limbed man in a white coat that tickles his ankles, which are exposed by his too-short trousers. Round bifocals with inch-thick lenses magnify his eyes. His frizzy hair reaches for the sky as if he'd stabbed one too many sockets this morning. He's certainly a gawky fellow, to say the least, perhaps the kind of guy to keep his seatbelt fastened at a drive-in movie.

But that voice... It sends shivers down my spine, then all the way back up. Deep as a bassoon, with a sense of authority, it practically wraps itself around me like a snake. The voice of God Himself.

I realize I've been standing in silence for an uncomfortable ten seconds. "I... Hello, sir," I manage.

The man nods once, and his hair bobs forward like a wet sponge. "How do you do? Are you new in town?"

I clear my suddenly-cobwebbed throat. "Yes, sir. You see, my car. I'm having a bit of trouble..." I gesture down Main and past the city limits, vaguely toward my shell of a Ford. The lanky man cocks an eyebrow as he listens—and a coldness taps me on the shoulder.

Had he been standing behind me the whole time? Could *he* be what had frightened the businessman?

"Well, I have a telephone just inside. Would you care to use it?"

My feet are quickly fused to the ground again. The man must see my reaction, because he shakes his head, embarrassed, and chuckles.

"I'm sorry, ma'am, I must seem pretty kooky right now, popping out of nowhere, right?" He adjusts his glasses and straightens his posture, casting a rail-thin shadow over me. He must be at least six-foot-six. "I run this little shop."

I glance again at the signage of his "shop," grandly pronouncing itself the mortuary of the entire county. Then, there's the piece of cardboard, making a mockery of the whole thing in immaculate penmanship.

The doc follows my gaze. "To paraphrase Oscar Wilde: Life is too important to take seriously. I feel the same way about what comes after."

I look back at him. "You read Wilde?"

A smirk. "I have more down-time than I know what to do with. So yes, I read anything I can get my hands on. My name is Dr. Milt O'Connor. And you are?" He extends a hand.

"Ramona." I smile and shake his hand. It's cold, as if he'd been holding a beverage for a long time, but kind and sincere.

"It's nice to meet you, Miss...?" He fishes for a last name.

"The pleasure's mine." I give his hand one last pump, definitively keeping my surname to myself for the time being.

The doc catches my signal. His smile is good-natured, and I see that his bottom teeth overlap crookedly like old wooden fence posts. I return his smile, but the chill from the shrouded sun keeps me alert.

"So would you like to use my telephone?"

"I..."

Should I trust this strange doctor? His grin appears genuine, but the suited businessman had seemed to fear the very sight of him.

"There are no auto mechanics here in Crawford," he continues, "but I have the number for the very best man for the job. He's up in Ellis County, not too far off."

The cloud passes and a sliver of sunlight catches the doctor's eyeglasses, turning the lenses into yellow discs. In that moment, he looks like a grinning jack-o-lantern, fire illuminating his eyes from within.

After the trying morning I've had—what with the car, the specters, the cold rejection of OKC and the eerie snowglobe that is Crawford—this strange mortician's kindness is a welcome change. I find myself relaxing and saying, "Yes, doctor, I'd appreciate that."

He smiles as if I'd just made his day. He turns, opens the door wide, and gestures for me to walk through. The frizzy hair atop his head reminds me of the tiny hats bellboys wear in fancy hotels, and I can't help it but chuckle as I enter.

"Welcome to my humble abode."

Plush carpet softens my footsteps, and scarlet curtains adorn the windows, making this place look more like the aforementioned hotel than a small-town mortuary. A staircase on the far side of the room leads to a second floor.

It's all a bit jarring—I'd had visions of dead bodies and bloody bags, not soft lighting and... Is that a hint of lavender?

The doc follows me in and closes the door, shutting out Crawford. "Can I offer you a drink? Juice, coffee, Coca-Cola?"

"Umm, water?"

"Of course." He steps past me.

I crane my neck upward. "Your abode, you say? You live here?"

O'Connor nods, his glasses sliding down his nose. "Yep. I have a small living quarters upstairs. Washroom, stove, bed, reading light. It's all I really need." From a cabinet, he withdraws a glass bottle of Malvern drinking water. "From the granite hills of England. Only the best for my guests."

His voice is as deep and wide as the Grand Canyon, but his awkward physique and ill-fitting clothing remind me of the begrudging bachelors at my senior prom. These contrasts somehow work together, and I find him oddly endearing.

"Thank you very much." And I mean it. I take the bottle and drink, nourishing my scratchy throat. I hadn't realized how parched I am.

"You're welcome, Miss." He pauses for a moment, then abruptly switches back to the previous conversation, like a record that had to be flipped over for the B-track. "The quarters upstairs are a bit too stuffy for my liking. I actually spend most of my time in the king's suite here on the ground floor." He gestures to another door, this one tucked in a corner and hidden by shadows. "I rarely go out because I'm so...buried in my work, you might say." He hiccups a laugh at his little joke.

"The king's suite?"

"Mhmm. Back there is where my A-list clients spend the night until it's time for them to climb down that six-foot ladder."

"Wait. Behind that door is—"

"Are," the doc quickly corrected. "Behind that door, there *are* multiple dead bodies lying in large metal drawers."

His bluntness catches me off guard. "I thought you looked on the funny side of death."

"What can I say? I'm a complex fellow." O'Connor laughs, which shakes the entire building. "Yes, this is just the lobby of the mortuary, where the architect felt the need to lull visitors into a sense of safety and pleasantry before opening this door and entering reality."

With a flourish, O'Connor pushes a palm against the door and floats through it. I follow, completely entranced.

He wasn't exaggerating—stepping from the plush, womb-like anteroom into the morgue proper is like entering another realm entirely.

The floor is tiled in a checkerboard pattern, the walls a tired, smudged plaster—I definitely don't want to know what the smudges are. Reflective metal tables sit in the corners, holding rulers, pencils, and all sorts of menacing instruments that make my skin crawl. A few lamps with adjustable necks eye me as I enter: watchdogs sensing a trespasser with equal parts aggression and curiosity. Harsh lightbulbs in iron cages dangle from the ceiling, bathing the room in a dull whiteness. The whole thing feels airy and ethereal, like a dream. Or a nightmare.

But the drawers are what immediately capture my attention:

Dozens of little square doors are affixed to the walls, stacked three high, hinges well-worn but sturdy, each with a handle like a refrigerator's.

And locks. Why do these drawers have locks?

They're numbered from *001* to *085*, wrapping around the room, a perfect circle of death. Surrounding me. A boa constrictor.

"Breathe, Miss." The doc places a gentle hand on my shoulder.

I hadn't realized I was holding my breath. I exhale, but my chest is still tight.

"These are my houseguests." He nods toward the drawers. "Unique in every way: who they were, their occupations, their passions, their vices, how they went belly-up..." He paces as he chats, flexing his fingers with nervous energy. "But they all converge here, and now, they're all nothing more than sacks of flesh stowed away for safekeeping, waiting to take a little dirt nap."

I shudder, and not just from the chilly draft. "These were people. Why are you so nonchalant about their deaths?"

"Because it's the way of life, Miss. People cloak the monstrous in euphemisms. They call it 'unspeakable' or 'unthinkable'—designations that are true simply because in using them, we make them so. But death isn't unthinkable. It happens millions of times every single day. And the sun still rises."

"But isn't it sad to see people who were once so... I don't know, so *human* reduced to inanimate objects on a slab?"

The doc's shoulders deflate slightly. "Everything ends, Miss." He turns his head left, then right, taking in all the drawers in his care. An impish smile tugs at his lips. "Number 16," he says as he nods to the metal drawer, "was a clown."

"Well, that's not very nice."

"No, I mean he wore white makeup, baggy pants, and danced around with elephants. And he was a buffoon too. Stupid, I mean. Stood on a rocking chair to try and adjust a crooked painting. Leaned too far one way, flailed like a seagull for a moment, went airborne, and the rest is history."

He huffs through his nose, as if he'd finished running a great distance. His recovery is quick, though, and he goes on:

"Number 33. A Klansman from Georgia, passing through on his way west. Roughed up a few innocent gentlemen on the way. He also kicked a puppy, I believe. He was asleep in a motel when a vessel burst inside his brain. Didn't feel a thing. Simply slipped away. No one has claimed his body. No one wants him, but his passing was quite peaceful."

He spins on the sole of his shoe, looking from one side of the room to the other. His white coat swirls around him like a cape. Odd—I don't recall any superheroes as fascinated with death as he is.

"Number 64. He was in his early thirties, the prime of his life. Exercised, ate a good balance of fruits and meats, never touched a drop of alcohol nor a puff of nicotine. He tithed to his church every Sunday, refused to say an ill word of any person he met—especially his lovely wife and two adoring sons. Was on the board of the Oklahoma Children's Hospital. Oh, I forgot to say he was a surgeon who volunteered at clinics on the weekends.

"Did he simply slip away like those other two dingbats? Nope. Cancer blossomed in his small intestine. He wasted away from the inside out for years. *Years*. His family watched. His friends mourned. He was in absolute agony, wondering why God was letting this happen. Eventually, he passed on, only after three surgeries and losing nearly fifty pounds.

"Yet, here they all are, under the same roof, reaching the same fate, booked for the same trip on the Gravesend bus."

As numb as I am with disbelief, I can't refute a single word he's said.

"The euphemisms and synonyms are all well and good, I suppose. But death is an inevitable part of this life, whether we choose to accept it or flee from the very thought of it. We're raised to see it as a tragedy, but it comes for each and every human. Many don't accept it, and that simply leads to an existence of fear and bitterness."

I ponder his last statement. "Why do you say that?"

"Well... Imagine denying that gravity exists. Or the wind. Something that others see as plainly obvious. Every time an apple falls from a tree or clouds move across the sky, your paradigm would be proven wrong. You'd be angry, resentful, and fearful of what else you're wrong about."

"Wow. That's...an incredible view of life, Dr. O'Connor. Or death, rather."

"Milt," he corrects genially.

I look up at him. "Dr. O'Connor, I hate to sound rude, but where's the telephone? It's been a long day."

He nods once. "Certainly. It's just on this far table." He gestures across the room to a boxy telephone, the numbers worn off its dial from years of use. "The number of the automobile mechanic I mentioned earlier is written on a tag pinned to the wall. I'll give you some privacy." He tips his head and bows out of the morgue, leaving me alone.

Well, alone, plus a few dozen chilled corpses tucked in their beds.

I clear my throat and take a breath, doing my darnedest to focus on the black telephone rather than the unseen—but incredibly present—bodies. Like a rook across a chessboard, I move directly to the metal table, refusing to even acknowledge the drawers.

I pick up the telephone's receiver and lean in to read the slip of paper tacked to the wall:

"*Scott, mechanic...*" followed by a letter and five digits.

I pause.

That's the only thing written on the note. Why did the doc have this mechanic's number pinned right here?

As if waiting for me?

Suddenly, I want nothing more than to leave Crawford. Leave the mortuary building. Leave this godforsaken room of death. With a trembling finger, I turn the dial for the corresponding number, press the receiver against my face, and wait.

A sharp musical note prods my inner ear.

And another.

And another.

My lungs feel smaller than seashells, unable to hold a full breath. Beads of sweat slide down my back, but they feel like slimy fingers caressing my flesh. I shiver and tighten my grip on the telephone.

I tap my fingernail against the metal tabletop. It sounds like a ticking clock. Or a time bomb...

What's taking so *long*?!

At last, a female voice responds: "I'm sorry, this telephone number is currently unavailable." It's a cold and mechanical voice, like an actress reading a script for the first time. "If you would like to hang up and try a different number—"

I pound my palm on the table and hiss, "You've gotta be kidding me!"

The robotic female voice continues, "Now, now, Ramona, there's no need to get emotional."

My blood freezes.

"Go, Ramona. You must go. Accept it."

The mechanical voice's threat hits me like a slap.

"Don't turn around either."

Then, static. The voice has hung up.

I'm stiff as a board. The white lights seem to intensify, making me squint, churning my stomach. The table's legs cast shadows across the floor, thin like prison bars.

Don't turn around...

I still my heartbeat to listen. The morgue is silent. The air vibrates with an electric charge, as if holding its breath. Waiting.

Tick.

A footstep. Someone is behind me. Some*thing*.

I need to turn, to leave, to run out of this sanitarium nightmare. But I'm rooted, clutching the telephone receiver, staring at the smudged wall.

Another *tick*. It's still there. I hear a slow, almost imperceptible inhale. For a moment, I think I may have imagined it, my frenetic brain trying to push me over the edge.

But then, an exhale.

Now. The time to move is *now*.

I grit my teeth, throw down the receiver, which springs back up thanks to its knotted cord. I spin to face the exit.

Nothing.

I groan. Wow. All these years of running from specters has altered my mind.

Regardless, this place still gives me the heebie-jeebies. I head for the door, stepping across the checkerboard tiles with no regard for the game rules.

Tick. Behind me again.

A skeletal hand grabs my shoulder. Frigid. Coarse. Strong. Before a scream can escape my throat, it yanks me around.

I'm face to face with an old woman who seems to only be half-there, like when I put the radio's dial between two stations. The deep wrinkles of her face seem to be filled with dust and flecks of copper. She pulls me close, with surprising power in her frail fingers, so that I'm centimeters from her ravenous maw.

Her breath. I almost gag. The stench of an ancient crypt.

She clacks her corn-kernel teeth together and croaks, "Leave this place." Her eyes flare with the intensity of an exploding sun, then blacken like charcoal.

I want to yell, kick, flee, but my limbs are paralyzed. A specter has never so much as looked at me, much less attack and shriek like this.

She bellows, "*NOW!*"

My knees buckle, but the old woman's grip keeps me on my quaking feet. Her craggy voice becomes a siren, wailing until my ears become numb. The medical instruments tremble on their tables, and the very walls pulse inward.

Then, the door flies open. The lanky doctor with the white coat bounds in. He glares directly at the old woman and balls his fists.

Even amid the horror, I realize something:

No one else has ever seen a specter. Until now. Until Milt O'Connor.

"You," he growls, the voice of God unleashing His wrath, "release her!"

The old woman's smoldering eyes snap from me to O'Connor, narrow and defiant. Her gaunt fingers release my shoulder, and I crumple to the floor. She stands tall and moves toward him, her wrinkly scowl contorting until her cheeks stretch beyond her face.

But O'Connor doesn't flinch. "I don't fear you. Go."

At that word, the woman stops immediately, twitches once, and sinks into the checkerboard floor. In an instant, she's gone.

Once again, the morgue is still. Deathly still.

O'Connor runs to where I've collapsed on the floor. He kneels and helps me into a sitting position. "Miss, are you alright?"

I stare at him slack-jawed, barely capable of stringing a sentence together. "You saw her. Do you see them?"

"I see them, yes. All of them." He adjusts his bifocals.

"How did you command her to leave?"

"Years of practice. Come, Miss, let's get you on your feet." He shifts to a squat, places his hands under my elbows, and we rise together. I nearly throw my arms around his torso in gratitude.

"Thank you, Milt." Tears poke the backs of my eyes, but I rein them in and smile instead. The first genuine smile I've had in a long time. "I just... I've never met anyone else who can see these... Well, I call them the specters."

We move out of the morgue's harsh light, back into the lobby with the plush carpets and scarlet curtains. Still, bile coats the inside of my throat, a foul reminder of the attack I just escaped—or, really, I was just rescued from.

O'Connor nods, his mop of hair bobbling. "Yes. These beings, these people..."

I shudder and eye the door to the morgue. "That was no person."

"You'd be surprised. I've been dealing with these things for a long, long while. They're trying to get by, just like you and me."

I cock an eyebrow. "You *sympathize* with them?"

He mulls over the question, swirling it like brandy in a snifter. "I can see where they're coming from. They're lost and confused. Imagine if you were forced into a realm you didn't understand, a dimension you may not have even believed in. How would you react if you were doomed to walk the night and confined to fast in fires?"

The literary reference scratches an itch I hadn't known was there. "Thanks, Hamlet," I smirk.

The doc grins too. "I knew you'd catch that little snippet." His deep voice sobers again. "Honestly, though, Miss, there's a vacant room upstairs. I think you should stay here until your car is fixed and you can get on the road again."

I'm taken aback. "Really? You want to give me a room?"

O'Connor stutters and suddenly looks self-conscious. He holds out a hand to stop me, then steps ahead to face me directly. The sunshine from the front window ebbs behind him. "Just as a friend, I swear.

I didn't mean it in that way." His words tumble out like he's trying to dam a river with over-explanation. "I just think we should look after one another. Plus, there's already another tenant up there. An old fellow named Gunner, completely harmless. There are two spare bedrooms—he's in one, you'll have the other. And my quarters are just down the hallway. You wouldn't be alone."

His embarrassment makes me giggle. I smile up at him. "Sure, Milt. I appreciate it." I put on a mockingly stern face and raise a finger. "Just no funny business," I tease.

He doesn't realize I'm kidding and nods. "Of course, Miss Price."

Another chill.

Another realization.

I never told him my last name.

The doctor continues to smile at me, eyes big and wide, his teeth gleaming as if polished. But my mind is in a cold sweat.

Who is this man? How does he know my name? Why is he helping me? Suddenly, although he doesn't change physically, everything about the man is different.

His white coat is sinister. The eyes behind the bifocals probe instead of beam. His deep voice isn't God's anymore—it's a demon's.

There's only one thing now:

Run.

I scan the lobby for an escape. But O'Connor has positioned himself between me and the only exit. Sneaky fellow.

I bend my mouth into a small smile to keep him from getting suspicious. "So where's this room, doc?"

What's his endgame, his goal? Why is he—

I shut off my mental inquisition. I need to get out of here first.

Where will I go—

Shut up and focus, Ramona.

Okay, he's facing me, and it doesn't look like he's caught wind of my suspicion. Good. The mortuary's exit is about twenty feet away. But I'd have to bob and weave around him to get there, and his spaghetti arms will ensnare me for sure. Can't get out that way. Yet.

The door to the morgue is just a few steps behind me. Nowhere to go or hide in there, and the telephone doesn't seem to want to cooperate. That's a dead end. In more ways than one.

That leaves upstairs. The staircase is diagonal from my position. I'll get him to lead me there, keep my charade up for the moment. Maybe I can take cover somewhere and wait for the doc to give up and leave. Or maybe I can shimmy out a window. Or perhaps the old man Gunner could help me. I need *something*, though—this is my only option.

O'Connor tilts his head toward the stairs. "Right this way. I'll show you, then we can go collect your bag from your car."

I hadn't told him about leaving my luggage behind either.

I giggle to cover up my frayed nerves. "I'll follow you!"

Too cheery. He'll notice for sure. He'll snap and become feral and throw me in one of his big metal drawers.

But he simply nods and holds out his arm toward the stairs. "After you. I insist."

Alright, then. It takes all of my concentration to lift my legs and walk at a natural pace. I want to run like a maniac, sweeping my foot under O'Connor's stilts as I go, but I need to keep my head on straight.

The white coat floats directly behind me: a specter wearing a fleshy disguise. Step by creaky step, I work my way up the stairs. The lights from the lobby fade behind us as we move upward, toward the darkened second floor. Shadows lengthen, the air bites my exposed skin, and static buzzes in my ear.

We're almost to the top. I can see the second floor. It consists of a short hallway with three doors: two on the left, one on the right. O'Connor said his residence was very small, so I deduce his room is on the left. I'm not sure which room is Gunner's—I'll have to follow my gut.

"Why did you stop, Miss?"

I hadn't realized it, but I've halted at the top of the staircase, legs locked like an Olympic sprinter just before the starter pistol. The doc is a few steps behind and below me. I gulp and make my move.

I lift one leg and twist, smacking O'Connor in the jaw with my heel. It's a solid hit, trembling all the way up my body and undoubtedly leaving quite the bruise on the doc's face. He doesn't cry out, instead falling backward down the stairs. I don't wait to watch him tumble like a runaway boulder—I race up the remaining stairs and pause in the hallway.

Which door?

The seconds tick by. Precious seconds. O'Connor will be back any moment, and he'll know my mindset is less than compliant.

The lone door on the right. That one. I dart toward it.

A terrifying fact I barely realize:

I hadn't heard O'Connor land at the bottom of the staircase. I didn't even hear him hit the ground. No thumping, no tumbling. As if he never touched the floor.

Go. Run.

I lunge for the door handle and scarcely manage to turn it before barreling into the bedroom.

It's arctic in here, instantly numbing my hands. And pitch black. Even though the door is still ajar behind me, no light seeps in from the hallway. I rub my palms together to generate some warmth, but I can't even see them through the inky shadows. And the static buzzing intensifies.

A purple light suddenly emanates from the room, and the glow stings my retinas. I turn to leave, figuring this room is a waste of my few remaining seconds.

The door slams shut, booming in the small, dark space. Like a tomb.

I grasp the doorknob and instantly recoil. It's searing hot, despite the frigid air.

I've had just about enough of Crawford.

Gritting my teeth, I look back at the violet glow, which radiates from an easy chair in the middle of the room. I crane my neck for a better look, but the high back of the chair blocks my view of whatever's sitting within.

Inch by inch, I orbit around the chair. The purple glow bathes the room in an alien shade, morphing a common bedroom into a scene from a dime science-fiction novel. The blacks are blacker, and all other colors—my dress, my skin, the floor—are a strange hue, from another dimension entirely. And the buzzing noise is starting to make my eyes twitch.

I finally circle around to the front of the chair. Within its fold sits an old man, head bowed to his chest. He's dressed in corduroy trousers, a dusty old shirt, and worn-out suspenders. A moth-eaten tweed cap hides his face.

He's withered, bent like a tree that has withstood decades of torrential winds. His clothing hangs from his thin frame. His hands lie on the armrests like the Lincoln Memorial, and he's just as statuesque, not moving, shifting, or even breathing. This must be Gunner, O'Connor's elderly guest.

Purple light emits from his skin like an ethereal lantern. I can hardly believe my eyes, but as I stare and stare, it doesn't change. I clear my throat and do my best to sound confident when I say his name: "Gunner?" I don't succeed at the confident part.

His hands jolt as if I'd awakened him from a deep slumber. Then, his head begins to rise. Slowly. Very slowly, a coffin's lid gradually creaking open.

I see his face. I stagger backward and stifle a scream.

His skin is waxy and creased into an eternal scowl, revealing teeth as black as obsidian. Wisps of lavender hair frame his face, wavering in an invisible breeze.

His eyes rest upon me. Eyes filled with fog, a broiling storm staring directly into my soul.

For years, I'd wished these specters would simply look at me.
I was foolish.

"What do you want?" His voice is coarse and reedy—the voice of a tobacco addict. It thunders with absolute malice, shaking the earth.

My heart hammers as if I'm already running, but my feet don't budge. I'm trapped in his purple glow, his misty gaze.

"How dare you," he rasps, his hands pushing against the armrests. He lurches to his feet, his stormy eyes never wavering from me. "You come in here, trying to drag me down *there*." Spite drips from the last word. "Did he send you? I'll betcha he did, that soulless devil."

His odious glare strangles me as he stands to his full height. The violet light shifts with his movements like a cyclone, swirling around the room and shepherding us closer together without either of us taking a step.

"I'll never leave, ya hear? You'll have to lug my cold body outta this room. No matter what that putz downstairs says, I'm staying put."

He keeps drawing nearer, and despite his monstrous appearance, I'm spellbound. The light zips around us with a mind of its own.

But I have no idea what he's talking about, and I open my mouth to say as much. "I—"

"*No!*" Purple light explodes outward as he bellows. The noise reverberates as if we're in a cavern. His jaw elongates, teeth gleaming like bullets. "*You know nothing!* Run back to that nocturnal demon in his white cloak and tell him..." His feet lift from the floor, and the violet glow turns into a supernova. "*I'LL NEVER LEAVE.*"

A bolt of lightning streaks across the room.

Finally, I scream. I run. I barge through the door. Charge down the stairs two at a time.

I'm back in the lobby, dim and gloomy now, the thick curtains drawn across the windows. My hair sticks to my skin with frantic sweat, my heart pounding in my chest like a piston, almost shattering my ribcage. O'Connor isn't in sight—I don't know where he is, but I almost don't care. I just need to run.

I trample the rich carpeting as I rush to the exit and grab the handle. It won't turn. I snivel and lean all of my weight against the door, but it's like beating my fists against a stone wall.

The windows. I grab a blood-red curtain with both hands and rip it down. I almost retch.

Where once there was an opening to the town of Crawford, there are now gray cinderblocks. The mortar is old and cracked—as if it's been there for decades.

I'm trapped.

My brain knows it's futile, but I punch the cinderblocks with all my might. My bones thump against the solid brick, but I feel no pain. I scream but hear nothing. I call out for help.

Call?

An idea:

The telephone.

It's worth a try. I'm desperate at this point, not thinking logically. I spin and run back into the cold, austere morgue.

The drawers and lamps glower at me, surprised to see me back so soon. So am I. The checkerboard tiles distort my vision, twisting and turning as if I'm tumbling down Alice's rabbit hole.

The phone, Ramona. Just get the phone.

But it's not there anymore. The metal table where it once sat now holds a different item: a yellowed newspaper, its corners curling like a beckoning finger.

My heart slows, along with my breathing, curiosity mixing with fear.

Even from across the room, I can see a monochrome photo on the front page. It's of a girl. A woman. I know who it is, but I deny it. Even as I shuffle closer, I refuse to see what's directly before me.

But it is what it is. She is who she appears to be. The hair, the build, the face shape and expression.

It's me. My photo accompanies a headline: *"Woman killed in collision."*

"Ramona." The deep, rumbling voice of God. Behind me. Soft and tender. Like a father breaking bad news to his child.

I turn to look at him. The eyeglasses. The frizzy hair. The white coat and ill-fitting slacks. I can describe him down to the most minute detail, yet I know nothing about who this man is.

In his hands, he holds a file, gently, as if it might crumble in the air like a dandelion. He opens it and reads: "Ramona Price. Twenty-one years old, born October 12, 1934." He practically whispers, forcing me to lean in, to listen. As if he's opening my hand, giving me the words, and closing it up again.

I know what he's going to say next, but still, it slaps me.

"Died July 2, 1955. Head-on automobile collision in Oklahoma City. Driving a dirt-brown 1935 Ford Coupe." He closes the file and lowers his eyes, almost ashamed, disheartened to be the one telling me this.

I take a ragged breath. "I'm dead." It's not a question.

O'Connor says, "I'm sorry, Ramona. It's..." He struggles to form the next sentence in his head. "Miss Price, I'm afraid it's not 1955. The year is 2025."

"I..." My knees begin to shake, but I quickly still them. I refuse to show my fear. "*I'm* the specter."

O'Connor dips his head further in a solemn nod. "The beings you see walking around you, the ghosts wearing clothing and jewelry you find strange, these specters that straddle their world and yours... These are real. *They* live in the physical world. They are people going about their lives, oblivious to your presence...for the most part."

The man in the street earlier today. The one who'd blanched and yelled, "*Stay away!*" He'd seen me. He'd thought I was a ghost. A specter.

Which I am.

I look at O'Connor, straight into his bespectacled eyes. "You. Are you...?" I can't even say it. It's too ridiculous, too childish, too insane. I gesture to the drawers.

The doc chuckles lightly. "I may not have a black robe or a scythe, but yes. That's me." His wry smile disappears. "I'm sorry, Miss. Truly, I am."

"What am I doing here?" Suddenly, I'm tired. Exhausted. So, so exhausted.

"When a human dies but doesn't accept it, they're left behind. Trapped halfway between realms. Doomed to walk the night, confined to fast in fires. But when they realize the truth, they can move on. Upgrade to the king's suite. I do what I can to help the lost find their way."

The electric lights sputter in their iron cages. Otherwise, it's silent.

He continues on: "The old woman in the morgue, Gunner upstairs... They've been here for decades. Just as I said earlier, not accepting death leads to an existence of fear and bitterness. In their ghostly forms, these negative emotions have distorted them, transformed them into the beasts you encountered. I thought, maybe, seeing them could help persuade you."

"Persuade me?"

I freeze. I see where this is going.

"Don't be like them, Ramona. Angry, resentful, fearful. Please."

I wipe a hand across my eyes.

2025... My family is dead. My friends are gone. Even if I wanted to venture out from this place and find them, I couldn't—no one can see me. And if they do, they see a spirit, something to be feared.

My head feels as if it's rapidly emptying, like it's rotting from the inside out. I clench my temples between my palms.

Then, a scraping sound. Metal on metal. I turn and see that O'Connor has pulled an empty drawer out from the wall. He stands next to it, hands clasped before him. Dutiful, but with kind eyes. He glances at the steel slab, then back to me.

"Ready, Miss Price?"

2

Tooth and Claw

Freaky Factor: 3/3

RUN, Tabitha told herself. *Don't look back. Don't do anything except put one foot in front of the other.*

The full moon illuminated her steps as she sprinted through the woods. Branches drew jagged lines across the night sky, like a witch's fingers reaching down to grab hold of her and never let go. Roots and dirt clods tried to trip her, but she couldn't stop. Couldn't slow down.

She knew that if she paused for even a moment to think of a plan, or to look for another escape route, or to climb a tree, she was done for. Her world would be ripped apart by claws and teeth. The last thing she'd hear would be the tearing of flesh from bone.

So she ran.

The werewolf's paws pounded the ground right behind her. She could smell its oaky fur and hear its coarse breath as it gave chase.

This ferocious beast had been pursuing her ever since the full moon rose above the horizon. She wanted to fall to her knees and cry out, *Why me?* Why had this monster chosen her? She was an innocent bystander, a regular person. She drove to work everyday, paid her taxes, visited her relatives, and lived a normal life. It just didn't make any sense.

But the beast didn't care what made sense or didn't. Its heavy footfalls never wavered, and its breath didn't fade away.

Tabitha ran all the faster. As much as she wanted to peek over her shoulder to see the terrible monster, she didn't. She was afraid she'd slow down just enough, and the beast would close its jaws around her head, and that would be the end.

But as fast as she was running, she was getting tired even faster. Her legs grew heavy, and an iron band of fatigue tightened around her chest. She wouldn't be able to keep this pace much longer.

Just as she was about to give up, she spotted something up ahead. She focused her eyes to see better in the moonlight. It was a squat wooden structure, with a slanted roof.

A cabin! Its walls looked thick and solid, with a single wooden door leading in or out. It should be a safe place...she hoped.

And even if not, it was the only choice she had.

Tabitha pushed her legs to go just a bit faster. When she sped up, the werewolf's ragged breathing did the same. She could hear its claws ripping through the soil, digging a grave with each step. As determined as she was to get away, it was just as determined to catch her.

The cabin was only a few feet away.

She reached out her hand.

Grasped the cold metal doorknob.

Flung open the door.

Fell into the cabin.

And slammed the door behind her. She scrambled to her feet and locked the deadbolt tight.

She leaned against the door, expecting the beast to try to ram it down. But the forest was silent. The only sounds were her own frantic breaths, the creaking of the floorboards beneath her feet, and the indifferent chirps of crickets outside.

Where was the monster? Had she lost it? Or was it waiting just on the other side of the door, ready to pounce as soon as she tried to leave?

She had to look outside to check. A window was cut into the front wall of the cabin, and she crept toward it.

Her heart felt like it was about to burst from her chest. She set a hand on one side of the window...leaned forward to glance through...

...and the werewolf glared right back at her. Its beady red eyes narrowed at the sight of its prey. Tabitha shrieked at the top of her lungs, shredding her throat in horror. The werewolf roared in response, fogging the glass of the window. Its teeth were like yellow daggers, with strands of saliva rippling against the force of its fury.

Tabitha dropped to the floor. She couldn't flee anymore. She was weary, yes, but mostly, she was too terrified to move. She rolled herself into a ball and cowered beneath the window.

She didn't budge all night.

Finally, tendrils of sunlight seeped under the door. Morning arrived, filtering through the canopy of treetops.

Tabitha hadn't slept a wink. Her body was stiff and achy, and it took her several tries to stand up. She rubbed her eyes and tousled her hair, which was a tangled mess. Her clothes were tattered, and her exposed skin was covered in scabs. Her crazed dash through the forest the night before had done a number on her.

Tabitha slowly got her bearings and prepared to leave. Hopefully the werewolf wasn't still out there. She crept toward the wall to peek outside.

But then she noticed...

The cabin didn't have a window.

Only a mirror.

3

A Halloween to Remember

Freaky Factor: 1/3

MAXINE GLANCED OUT the front window of her house. As the sun dipped below the horizon, the Halloween spirit officially stirred from its hibernation. All down the street, porch lights were turning on, many of them purple and orange. Inflatable jack-o-lanterns and cats sprang to life. She could sense the kids within their homes jittering with energy as they donned their costumes, ready to be unleashed upon the world.

The Halloween season had certainly been in full swing for several weeks, but tonight... *This* was the real deal. It wasn't all talk anymore. October 31st had arrived, and it was almost time for the most hallowed of All Hallows' Eve traditions: trick-or-treating!

Maxine loved everything about Halloween: the decorations, the movies, the vibes. But most of all, she loved trick-or-treating. Each year, she bought the best candy and decked out her porch. She always made a point of complimenting the kids' costumes, whether or not they were particularly good—few things made a kid smile more than being told they had an awesome Halloween costume.

She dumped all her candy into a big bowl and set it on a table in her entrance foyer. She was ready. "Bring on the trick-or-treaters!" she said to herself.

Trick-or-treating had been a big part of her childhood. It was the main reason she still loved Halloween as much as she did. There was something special about slipping into the skin of your favorite character, walking door to door, and demanding sweet treats from strangers. It all felt somewhat dangerous, but at the same time, it was publicly acceptable and totally safe. Like bungee jumping. That was how Maxine felt about Halloween in a nutshell: It was the one time of year society deemed it sane to take a few chances.

When she was a little girl, she always dressed up as the same thing. She would pull her messy hair into a bun, place a tiara on top, then don her ballet uniform and a pair of gossamer wings. Thus, she'd transform from plain ole Maxine into a majestic fairy queen.

A fairy *queen*—not a fairy princess. When adults handed out candy, they without fail asked her if she was a princess. For some reason, that irked elementary-aged Maxine to no end.

"Oh, what a pretty princess you are!" they'd all say.

Nowadays, Maxine would simply nod and let a misunderstanding like that pass on by. But not little Maxine. She stomped her ballet-slippered foot and asserted, *"I'm a fairy queen, thank you very much!"*

Even decades later, as she stood in her own house, Maxine chuckled and blushed slightly at the memories. She'd been such a stubborn little thing. It was a wonder her parents had allowed her to choose the same costume year in and year out.

Yes, Halloween after Halloween, the adults always assumed her tiara was that of a princess, not a queen.

Except for one lady. On the Halloween of Maxine's fifth grade year—the last Halloween of elementary school, before she graduated to middle school and the world as she knew it ended—she'd knocked on the door of a nice-looking house. The woman had been really friendly...but most of all, she'd rightly identified Maxine as a queen. She'd even given her two candy bars. None of that "fun-size" nonsense.

It had been a great night. Not only had it cemented her love of Halloween, but it also let her know that everything was going to be okay.

Maxine chuckled at the fun memory. She was surprised at how clearly she recalled that Halloween night. Just thinking about it made her smile.

The sound of footsteps snapped her out of her thoughts. Little feet were approaching her door from the outside. Someone was coming!

Tiny knuckles rapped against the door three times.

Maxine grinned as she picked up the candy bowl. Kids usually used the doorbell, but this trick-or-treater knocked. It showed confidence and determination. Maxine liked it.

Maxine opened the door and looked down at her first patron of the night. It was a little girl, with her untamed hair pulled up into a bun. A plastic tiara held her wild locks in place. She was clad in a pink leotard and tutu, ballet slippers, and butterfly wings tying the whole ensemble together.

Everything Maxine had been planning to say evaporated from her mind. Her mouth gaped open, as if she'd forgotten how to use it.

The girl beamed up at Maxine. "Trick or treat!"

Maxine cleared her throat. This girl's costume was a coincidence. Nothing more. Of course it was. Maxine silently chastised herself and smiled. She was being awkward, just standing there, staring at the little girl on her porch. She pulled herself together and greeted the girl with a friendly smile.

"Hello there!" she said. "I love your fairy queen costume!"

The girl giggled. "Thanks!" She twirled, her tutu and wings glistening in the porch light. "Everyone calls me a princess, even though I'm obviously a *queen*."

Maxine felt a chill. But not out of fear. She felt as though she were standing on the edge of a cliff, but she was harnessed to safety. Like she was about to bungee jump.

She tentatively said, "Well, I think you deserve two treats tonight." She fished two full-sized candy bars from her bowl and dropped them into the girl's basket.

The girl trilled, "Wow! Thanks, miss!" She turned on her slippered heel and bounded away. Her wings flopped with each step, as though she were moments away from taking flight.

Maxine watched her leave, clutching the candy bowl to her chest.

Had she...?

Was that...?

Maxine didn't know for sure what had just happened.

As the girl reached the street, she chattered with her friends: "Hey, guys! Check out what that nice lady just gave me! I don't think I'll get better stuff next year in sixth grade."

Even though Maxine's heart was racing, her smile grew. "Happy Halloween!" she called out.

The girl peered over her shoulder, her tiara barely restraining her messy locks. She waved, then skipped down the street.

Maxine watched the regal fairy queen disappear into the night. The girl had been right: She doubted next year's Halloween could possibly be better than this one. But she was determined to enjoy it while it lasted.

4

Haunted Animal House

Freaky Factor: 0/3

"WOW, TH-THAT PLACE looks s-s-scary!" bleated Sarah the Sheep. She wasn't embarrassed of her emotions and didn't mind telling her friends that she was nervous...but all the same, she tried to stop shaking. Her hooves knocked on the sidewalk, making her nerves even more obvious.

Her friends gathered around and stared up at the haunted house. This attraction was by far the most popular stop at the local fair. Dozens of critters streamed through the entrance, giggling and shoving one another in excitement.

Sarah craned her neck to see around the back of the house, wondering if those same animals were still so cheery when they exited the attraction. She couldn't quite see. But she definitely heard caws, squawks, brays, and roars coming from inside. Were they cries of fun? Sarah liked to think so. But still, her hooves clicked where she stood.

Carl the Camel gulped, forcing a thick knob of fear down his long throat. "Yeah, real scary!" Sarah didn't think he was agreeing with her just to make her feel better—he actually looked pretty nervous. In a roundabout way, that *did* make her feel better.

Bart the Badger and Rebecca the Rooster also nodded, both staring at the ominous house with wide eyes.

But Elliot the Elephant scoffed. "Scary?! I've eaten peanuts that are scarier than that place!"

Rebecca clucked, "You don't think it looks even a little spooky?"

"Not at all!" declared Elliot as he crossed his trunk in defiance. "Look at it! It's just a big set they built to try and mess with wimps like you guys. The cobwebs are fake, the zombies are cardboard cutouts, the lightning is just strobe lights... It's embarrassing, really."

Sarah lowered her head, trying to hide her worried expression.

Bart came to the group's defense: "Well, we *know* it's not real." He paused, then shot a quick glance to his friends, confirming the house wasn't actually haunted. Once they each gave him a quick nod, he went on. "But you can still be scared by something even if you know it won't hurt you."

Elliot huffed, ruffling everyone's fur and feathers with a great burst of wind. "I bet I won't be scared at all." With that, he stomped toward the entrance, ready to prove himself right.

"H-H-Hold on," Sarah said. She glanced up and down the sidewalk. "We should wait for Marvin." The friends had arrived at the fair earlier than Marvin, and they'd agreed to wait for him before doing any attractions.

Elliot raised an eyebrow and laughed. "Too scared to follow me?" He rumbled onward, joining the line of critters migrating into the haunted house.

Carl, Bart, and Rebecca shrugged at Sarah. They paused for a moment, waiting to see what she'd do.

With a small sigh—more to release the knot in her stomach than anything—Sarah tried to smile. The four animals timidly followed Elliot into the house.

Once they stepped inside, it was as though they'd been dropped into another world. The air was colder. The floor was unsteady. The walls pulsed with ghostly energy.

But Elliot muttered under his breath, "Air conditioning. Rickety floorboards. Hydraulic pistons." He snorted from his trunk.

On the other hoof, Sarah found herself having a good time. She was oddly grateful that Elliot was pointing out how the effects of the haunted house were done. If she knew the wicked chill was only a fan, that allowed her to enjoy the ride.

The friends moved through the haunted house, rounding every corner with gleeful caution. Ghosts popped out, drawing a screech from Carl. Spiders dropped from the ceiling, which caused Rebecca and Bart both to cower. Eerie music played throughout, which sent a chill through Sarah's wool. Inevitably, after each scare, they all laughed until they had to catch their breath.

Except for Elliot, who only rolled his eyes. "So lame," he sneered.

Finally, they reached the exit. Sarah no longer had to wonder what critters did as they walked out of the haunted house. She found out herself: They laughed and talked about their favorite parts.

"I liked the floating crystal ball," said Carl.

"And the barnyard graveyard scene!" added Bart.

"Ooh," Rebecca cawed, eager to jump in, "I liked the zombies! You can't have a haunted house without zombies."

Sarah said, "Th-That skeleton jump-scare really g-g-got me!"

Of course, Elliot rolled his eyes at her. He said, "It did? Really?! I wasn't scared at all. Not even the teensy-tiniest bit."

Just then, a voice squeaked, "Hi, guys! Sorry I'm late!" Marvin the Mouse skittered along the sidewalk toward the group.

Elliot's eyebrows shot skyward, and he reared back on his hind legs. His trunk whipped around as he shrieked in utter terror. He folded his huge ears around his face and curled into a ball, trying to hide from the teensy-tiny mouse.

Marvin glanced around, confused. "What was that all about?"

Elliot lifted an ear ever-so-slightly to peek out. "You really snuck up on me."

"Oh yeah," grinned Rebecca. "You, a huge elephant, are freaked out by a little mouse!"

The other critters started to cackle and point at Elliot in mockery...but Sarah said, "H-Hey, don't make f-f-fun of him. Everyone's sc-scared of something."

As the laughter died down, Elliot stood back up, lowering his ears fully. He smiled his silent thanks at Sarah.

Marvin looked up at his friends. "So what did I miss?"

Before anyone else could answer, Elliot said, "We just walked through a really scary haunted house. Wanna come through with us again?"

5

A Perfect Match

Freaky Factor: 1/3

THE SKY WAS AS BLACK as tar, with only a few pinpricks of light puncturing the darkness. All was quiet, the rolling hills and lush pastures blanketed in silence. The wooden blades of a windmill creaked slightly, but they quickly stilled themselves, as if ashamed of disturbing the peace. A faint breeze tickled the blade of grass, sending them into a faint dance, but they hardly made a sound.

The crickets didn't chirp. The owls didn't hoot. The wolves didn't howl. Even the creatures designed to rule the night were sleeping soundly.

The countryside was as motionless as a painting, as if created by an artist hoping to capture the essence of tranquility.

But in the nearby village of Peaceshire, it was a different story.

Screams cut through the air. Terror flooded the streets. Chaos reigned. Every man, woman, and child ran to and fro, back and forth, left and right, shrieking until their throats were raw.

Frank stomped along a cobbled road. He raised his arms threateningly as he walked. He curled his lip into a hideous snarl. He gnashed his tombstone-like teeth at the fleeing villagers.

He was a horrible monster, come to terrorize the people.

...Again.

One of the men pointed at him and yelled, "The horrible monster has come to terrorize the people! Again!"

Frank nearly rolled his eyes. Yeah, everyone knew that. It couldn't have been more obvious.

But he was a professional. He wouldn't let himself get annoyed. Not in front of the people he was supposed to be frightening. After a quick breath, he put himself back in full-fledged evil mode.

He released a baritone growl and held out his gnarled hands. The townsfolk screamed and fled anew, like fish in an aquarium that had been shaken.

Honestly, Frank was surprised the people of Peaceshire were still afraid of him. He'd been the terrorizer of his village for...

He did some quick mental math. Numbers weren't his strongest suit, so he had to pause his rampage while he thought.

At least ten years. For more than a decade, he'd been this village's dedicated monster, living in a shack behind one of the hills. Every seven days, he'd emerge, do some damage, growl at the people, and go home. This night was just like any other.

He marched into the open-air market. Luckily, the people had already retreated from there. He didn't like causing injuries, but he also didn't want anyone to catch onto that little detail.

Anyway, on with the monstering.

He knocked over food stalls, kicked holes through wagons, smashed pottery, and tore apart clothing... When he was done, the market was unrecognizable.

Just like when he'd ransacked the market last week.

And the week before that.

And the week before *that*.

Alone in the destroyed market, he allowed himself a sigh. After years of being a monster, it all felt so...simple. Easy. Routine. Shaking his head, he made his way toward the town square.

It was kinda funny: The townsfolk were bakers, butchers, harvesters, and artisans, with schedules and duties to perform. He had a job too. In a way, they weren't so different. But in other ways, they were quite different. Like how he was a deformed creature pieced together in a lab, designed to inflict pain and torment upon the world.

But other than that, they were pretty similar.

As he slunk toward the center of Peaceshire, a small mob of villagers gathered in front of him. They wielded pitchforks, clubs, and furrowed eyebrows.

Their leader called out, "We won't let you do this any longer, beast!" But his voice shook like a leaf in a storm.

Cute.

This happened every so often. A particularly stubborn townsperson, sick and tired of their wagon being kicked over every week, convinced enough people to form a cluster of resistance.

It never lasted long.

Frank eyed the mob before him. He considered taking a side-street, but they were blocking the quickest path to the town square, and he didn't feel like walking more than he had to. So he cracked the sutured joints in his neck and went to work

He snarled a little, stomped around, and shook his fists. Sure enough, the angry mob became a pile of crying babies, and they scattered immediately.

It had become a pattern he could do in his sleep. Yes, Frank enjoyed making people scream in horror. Of course he did. Who wouldn't?

But he yearned for more. He felt like he just wasn't reaching his full potential as a monster. There was more to life than knocking over carts and yelling at innocent villagers. Right?

As he stepped into the town square, a shroud of silence fell upon everything. The only sounds were his heavy footfalls echoing against the stone buildings around him. He glanced left, then right. No one was there.

Weird. Usually when he attacked, the townsfolk flocked here.

But not this time.

At that moment, a flame ignited across the square. Frank cringed and hid behind his hands—he hated fire! It was hot and bright, the two things he hated most of all. There was a reason he only emerged at night.

A man stepped across the cobblestones, his boots clicking like a drumbeat. He held a torch aloft, which illuminated his sharp, angular face.

"Stop right there!" bellowed the man. He had a strong voice, along with a venomous glare that actually made Frank nervous. "Your reign of terror is over!"

Frank felt something in his chest. Indigestion? No, that couldn't be it—he hadn't eaten in decades...

Could it be fear? Maybe a little. Frank hadn't felt scared in a long, long time. But that wasn't all.

There was a trill in his rotten heart. A spark. A glimmer. A sense of...hope.

As he beheld the man before him, Frank felt electricity in his veins, not unlike the lightning that had brought him to life so many years before.

At last, a worthy opponent! Someone who could make things interesting in Peaceshire.

The man waved his torch, preparing to do battle. Frank unleashed his mightiest roar, charged forward...and smiled. Finally, the monster had found his monster hunter.

6

Center Stage

Freaky Factor: 0/3

ANTOINETTE CREPT THROUGH the backstage area. She normally didn't want to bother anyone on a regular day, but this was no regular day—it was opening night! Actors and crew members scurried every which way, studying their dog-eared scripts, chattering in earpieces, or just muttering nervously to themselves.

The air was thick with anticipation. And nerves. And excitement. And a bit of dread. But that was typical on show nights. As much as everyone backstage loved theatre, they were scared to death of it at the same time. They treasured it and feared it all the more, sort of like a pet lion.

Or so Antoinette assumed. She wasn't an actress or part of the theatre staff. She just lived in the building.

She knew she should get out of everyone's way, but she couldn't resist sneaking a peek at the audience. She peered around the thick red curtain that currently shielded the bustling actors from the patrons taking their seats. The material was plush and velvety...again, so she presumed. As the theatre's resident ghost, she couldn't feel much of anything.

The auditorium was nearly full. Hundreds of people jostled in their seats, chatting excitedly and flipping through their programs. The electric lights faded and brightened a few times, signaling that the play was only a few minutes away from starting. The hubbub of the audience both intensified and quieted down as they braced for the show to start.

As the people in the auditorium settled in for the performance, the actors backstage grew even more frenzied. Antoinette couldn't help but giggle. She always enjoyed the hustle and bustle of performers getting ready.

The old theatre had been her home for hundreds of years, and as such, she'd watched countless shows on its stage. She'd seen rising stars become has-beens, geniuses be exposed as hacks, and amateurs turn into genuine artists.

As if on cue, one of the actors paced right by Antoinette. She didn't know his name or recognize his face, so he must be a newcomer. He was playing the show's narrator, so he had pages of lines to memorize. If his sweaty forehead and wide eyes were any indication, he wasn't feeling very confident. He murmured his lines under his breath, running them over and over. "Two households, both alike in dignity... In far Verona, where we play our scene..." He paused, then winced. "No! It's *fair* Verona." After checking his script, he sighed again. "And *lay* our scene... Oh no, I'm doomed."

Antoinette felt for the poor actor. She knew this play very well—it'd been produced in her theatre hundreds of times over the centuries, and she'd watched every performance. Still, she leaned over the actor's shoulder to gaze at the script in his shaky grasp.

The actor shuddered and looked around for the source of the sudden cold. "What in the world...?"

Antoinette gasped silently. She often forgot that she gave off a chilly aura. Not wanting to worry or distract the actor further, she drifted away, leaving him to his last-second rehearsal.

As she floated backstage, she wistfully whispered to herself: "The which, if you with patient ears attend, what here shall miss, our toil shall strive to mend." These were the concluding lines of the monologue the actor was going over. She knew them all by heart.

Despite her intangible existence, Antoinette had always dreamed of being an actress. She spent her infinite days watching the performers rehearse, and she usually memorized their lines along with them. She wanted to play every part, embody every character, and feel the roller coaster of emotions that came with acting.

But no one could see her. And very could even hear her. For an actress, that would be a fate worse than death.

Out in the auditorium, the lights dimmed fully. The spectators hushed. It was time for the show to start!

The curtain rose, removing the only barrier between the real world and the dreamland of theatre. The audience applauded, and with that, the performance began. Antoinette took her usual place in the rafters and smiled dreamily. She had the best seat in the house, without a doubt.

The narrator scuttled out onstage. He gulped and blinked a drop of sweat from his eyes. Antoinette was rooting for this newcomer. He'd been frightfully nervous backstage, but she hoped he'd rise to the occasion when the spotlights were upon him.

The narrator planted himself at the front edge of the stage. Ready to start the show with a bang, he looked out at the audience and opened his mouth...

But nothing came out. Not a croak, not a squawk, not a peep. He was utterly frozen.

Antoinette gasped, "Stage-fright!" She'd seen this phenomenon plague many performers over the years, but this was the worst case she'd ever witnessed. She whispered in encouragement, "Come on! You've got this!"

But the actor couldn't say a word. His eyes cast about frantically, as if searching for a life-preserver.

Antoinette dropped down from the rafters, invisible to the human eye, and hovered right next to him. The actor nearly shivered from the chill she emitted, but he was too frightened of the audience staring at him to move.

She quietly fed him the opening line: "Two households, both alike in dignity..."

The actor glanced over both shoulders, looking for the source of the soft voice that was helping him. When he saw he was alone onstage, he blanched in confusion.

Keeping her voice low and calm, Antoinette pushed, "Just breath. You'll do great."

"Umm..." He wiped his upper lip, which glistened under the spotlights. Finally, he cleared his throat and repeated the line in a mad dash, all as one word: "Twohouseholdsbothalikeindignity!"

Antoinette directed him, "Slow down. Pause after the next line."

Step by step, they made it through the opening scene together. When the narrator stepped aside to make way for the other actors, Antoinette floated away. A few minutes before each of the narrator's lines, she returned to his side. Each time, he shivered at her chill, but instead of being frightened, he seemed to feel comforted by the change in temperature.

And before she knew it, the show was over. She'd helped the newcomer through his first performance. During the curtain call, he even got the loudest applause.

Despite the fact that no one could see her, Antoinette took a bow. She wasn't a famous actress like she'd always wanted to be, but she'd helped someone else achieve their dream, and that felt pretty great.

And besides, maybe she didn't *have* to be an actress. She grinned—perhaps she had a knack for directing!

7

The Creatures' Tavern

Freaky Factor: 1/3

DANNY GULPED AND EYED the ramshackle old building warily.

He stood across the street, unsure what to do next. His heart and brain told him to run up to that building, burst through the door, and get to the bottom of this mystery.

But his feet wouldn't budge. It was as though his shoes were made of concrete, merged with the sidewalk. He couldn't move if he wanted to.

It was Halloween night, and his best friend Kayla wasn't answering his texts. They always hung out together on Halloween, but this year, she'd made a halfhearted excuse, saying she was going to stay home because she was "tired."

Throughout the day, he'd sent her messages, sharing funny memes he'd found or offering to bring her food. No response. This was extremely unlike Kayla, who never turned down a burrito delivery or had a neutral reaction to a meme.

Something was wrong.

He'd stopped by her house to see if she was okay, but she wasn't there. She'd lied to him about staying in for the night.

Something was *very* wrong.

He didn't want to impose, but desperate times called for desperate measures. He'd used the "share my location" feature they shared on their phones to find out where she was. Her photo had appeared as a dot on a map of the city, headed downtown. Danny had called and texted one last time, but she hadn't answered.

Was she sneaking out with other friends? Maybe she was sleepwalking around town? Had she been kidnapped? Horrible scenarios played through his mind, each more dire than the last. He had to make sure she was safe. So he'd followed her dot downtown.

The city was decked out for Halloween. People had streamed past him dressed as goblins, ghouls, and ghosts, but he'd paid them no mind. He'd only focused on locating Kayla. Her life could depend on it!

Finally, he'd caught up with her but kept his distance. She'd been walking with purpose, headed somewhere in particular—he could scratch sleepwalking off his list of theories.

Just a few minutes ago, he'd seen her disappear into this building. It was stout and tilted to one side, like a cake that had been sat upon. Cracked windows peered at him from across the street. Weeds grew from the dirt that encrusted the concrete steps leading to the front door. All in all, it was an eerie place, and he had no clue why Kayla would blow him off to come here.

She could be in danger. She could need his help, and he was simply standing on the sidewalk like a dummy.

Suddenly, his feet began to march forward. Thoughts of his friend in trouble overrode his fear of the building.

Not that he didn't find the place scary anymore. He very much did. But still, he crossed the street, pumping himself up. He could do this. He could handle whatever lay inside this creepy old building. He had to. For Kayla.

He stopped before the front door. It was just a normal, wooden door. Nothing to be frightened of.

He steeled himself, clenched his jaw, and threw it open.

What he found inside was like nothing he'd ever seen before.

Strobe lights and disco balls lit up the room. Streamers cascaded from the ceiling. Raucous music caused the walls to pulse with the beat. Tables were full of sweet treats and finger-foods. It was a Halloween party—a really *fun* party, by the looks of it. But it was the partygoers who made him stop and stare.

Ghouls and monsters were everywhere, laughing and partying. Banshees flew through the air. Goblins led the conga-line. Werewolves howled at the moon-shaped disco balls. A mummy manned the DJ booth, keeping the music alive.

There, in the middle of the dance floor, was Kayla. She was leading a cluster of monsters in some sort of jig that Danny had never seen before...but she was really good at it, and she seemed to be having the time of her life.

Danny ran up to her, slinking between the monsters. "Kayla!" he called over the dance music.

Kayla froze when she saw him, her smile disappearing. "Danny! Uh..." She awkwardly waved. "Hi!"

"What is this place?" he asked.

"Um..." She looked around, stalling as she tried to come up with a reasonable explanation. But the centaur serving slices of pumpkin pie didn't quite lend itself to a reasonable explanation. She sighed and told him the truth: "This is the Creatures' Tavern. We come here on Halloween to relax without being feared or judged."

Danny arched an eyebrow. "Wait, so... That means *you're* a creature?"

"Yeah," she answered, head slightly bowed. "I've wanted to tell you for so long, but I was worried. I didn't know how you'd take it."

Danny didn't respond right away, his nose pinched as he processed this life-changing information.

Kayla coughed a chuckle. "I mean, it wasn't like I was hiding it too hard. I've dressed up as a vampire for Halloween every year since we were little. You didn't find that suspicious at all?" She laughed again, trying to lighten the mood.

But Danny didn't laugh. He only frowned.

Kayla gulped. "Are you mad I didn't tell you?"

"Yes," he said. "But not about you being a vampire. I'm bummed no one told me about this awesome place!"

Kayla opened her mouth to ask what he meant. But at that moment, Danny became slightly transparent and began to float.

She gasped. "You're a ghost?!" Her surprise turned into a smile, which then morphed into full-fledged laughter.

Danny held out a shimmering hand. "Care to dance?" Kayla accepted his offer, and they drifted into the air together. She once again led the monsters in the jig, but Danny caught on quickly.

Everyone in the Creatures' Tavern cheered—the ghouls, monsters, goblins, werewolves, ghosts, and vampires—welcoming their newest patron.

8

Cronos

Freaky Factor: 3/3

DECEMBER 31, 1933
Yonkers, NY
10:06 p.m.

• • • •

IT'S HERE.

Something the world has never seen. And for good reason. If this monstrosity had lived in our realm, gotten a good taste for human flesh, acclimated to our atmosphere and environment and all that...our species wouldn't have made it past the Stone Age.

Stone Age. It all comes back to time, huh?

I peek out from behind the rear tire of my truck. Everything's totally still, except for the occasional wisp of frosty breath puffing from my lips. My teeth are chattering—it's freezing out here, and I didn't get the chance to grab my coat or gloves before leaving the tent. Running for your life can make you a bit forgetful.

But the coast is clear now. Not a person in sight. There are lines of empty cars belonging to the customers who've fled. Our boxes and crates are stacked in a pile about fifty yards away, also empty. A couple of floodlights—illuminating the field and our signs a few minutes ago—have been knocked on their sides, doing a bang-up job of brightening a few patches of dead grass. There's the huge tent that houses so many memories, so many shows over the years. The bright colors of the canvas look garish and sarcastic in the cold night.

I set my hands on my knees and try to quietly stand. But the cold has rusted my joints, and I fall back to the ground.

Panicked footsteps. Frantic breathing.

Janelle dashes out of the big-top tent, terror etched into her face. "*Run!*" she screams to the silent, indifferent sky. "Run before—"

It leaps out of nowhere. Truly nowhere. Its dark, scaly skin had camouflaged it against the bitter darkness, but now, it's roaring. Its jaws are open wide to reveal red, fleshy gums and rows of yellow teeth. It tackles Janelle, paws slashing and jaws gnashing, and feasts upon her.

In seconds, she's gone. Consumed.

I don't even have time to be horrified.

• • • •

• • • •

JANELLE HISSES MY NAME and beckons me over.

I'm standing just off stage-right, moments from starting today's matinee performance. I check my watch—yeah, right on the dot. I shake my head at Janelle and gesture toward center-stage. Showtime, I'm saying.

Janelle holds up a clipboard and taps it with a furious talon.

Uh-oh. Her clipboard. Bad sign.

When finances are low, she starts scribbling on that clipboard.

When finances are apocalyptic, she carries it everywhere.

A lump of granite plops in my gut, but I plaster on a smile and step out into the lights.

"Hello, hello, everyone!" I talk the way I think a showman does. "Welcome to our..."

My eyes adjust to the change in lighting and I see the size of our crowd.

So. Our tent is quite enormous, with a maximum capacity of 300 happy customers. If need be, it has the ability to be broken down and transported. But it never need be, to be honest. We haven't had a booking in years, out-of-town or otherwise. My predecessor's predecessor had purchased and painted this tent many decades ago, which must have been much more optimistic times for circus folk.

I'd joined the motley staff of Townshend's Shanty a few years back, in October of '29. Just my luck. A few days before we all found out Uncle Sam's pockets were filled with nothing but sand.

I'd come aboard after ditching my family in Vermont, hoping for excitement and adventure like I'd seen in the motion pictures. I was convinced anything was possible—turns out I was right, but I'd only imagined good things. Ten days after I was hired to sweep the floors, the ringleader announced we had no cash and vamoosed. I hear he's in Mexico now, but I bet he's actually just in Dover or Philadelphia.

One by one, people left the Shanty until I became the highest-ranking employee. Yeah, you try explaining it to me, cuz I still don't get it.

Times were tough for everyone, but especially two-bit local sideshows. You might think being close to New York City would be good for business, but it's a curse—if someone actually wants to see a show, they're far more likely to make the trip into Manhattan than hang around a small town on the outskirts. We only bring in enough cash to eat a meal-and-a-half a day, and our blankets have holes in them.

I bet it's the name. "Townshend's Shanty" doesn't exactly draw people in with promises of wonder and dreams. Apparently, this troupe was started by some old codger named Townshend back when New York still used money with King George's face on it. He died, no one changed the name, the Civil War happened, Wall Street went splat, and now I'm stuck with it.

So here I am: 24 years old, in charge of a limping circus and a tent big enough to be God's hairnet, acting as master of ceremonies (even though I have no stage presence) and manager (even though I have no leadership skills), smiling like a dope in front of six customers on a Monday afternoon.

Six. In a space big enough to hold... I do the math right quick... fifty times as many.

The New Year's crowd isn't as dense as I'd hoped. Or maybe it is, but in places that aren't here. No one wants to spend 1933 in a huge flamboyant tent called the Shanty.

I let out a groan but do my best to not make it noticeable. I adjust the ill-fitting ringmaster's jacket and hold out my arms. "Welcome all and one to Townshend's! I-I'm glad you could come. Spending your afternoon with us is...quite the treat. For us. And for you as well!" I sigh internally. P.T. Barnum I ain't.

But I soldier on, trying to imitate a showman rather than being one. "Within these walls, you will find amazing..." I whip my head across the mostly-empty bleachers—the six people are spread out, leaving oceans of empty seats between them. I grin sheepishly and drop the Barnum voice. "Can we all bunch in together on the front row here? No sense being all separate." The people look at each other for a moment. "Yeah, I'm serious," I laugh. "C'mon now, we gotta leave room for all the late-comers. But you were on time, so you get the front-row-treatment."

The people chuckle and slowly migrate to the front bench. There's a middle-aged guy, what looks like two high-school kids cutting class, an elderly gentleman, and a dad with his small son. They settle in side-by-side, smiling politely at one another.

I call over my shoulder, "Janelle, can we get a bag of peanuts for each of our guests? On the house. Water from the faucet too." I turn back to the audience. "I'll pay for the waters."

More laughs, a bit more comfortable this time.

"Well." I clear my throat and check the show order scribbled in ink on my sweaty palm. "First up, prepare to be amazed by our very own...Benvolio the Brave!" I pause, think, then make a last-second decision. "You, sir!" I point at the kid, probably about eight years old. "How'd you like to help Benvolio rip a Yellow Pages in half?"

The boy's face brightens instantly. "Wait, really?"

"If it's okay with your pops, step right up!"

The father nods, and the kid races to center-stage, vibrating in his shoes, flexing his bony arms like Atlas.

I scan the microscopic audience one more time—the dad, the high-schoolers, the two solo men, and, of course, the kid are all smiling ear to ear.

It feels good. So this is why I joined this place years ago.

• • • •

• • • •

THE TUESDAY MATINEE is slightly larger than yesterday's. Very slightly.

Eight people are in the audience today. Again, they naturally sit very far apart from one another, as if in quarantine.

Yesterday, after I'd given out snacks and brought the boy into the act, Janelle took me aside, told me I did a great job interacting with the audience, and said I can't do it again. Her eyes were heavy as she said it, but we can't give out food willy-nilly, and we can't get the reputation of letting kids break stuff with our strongman.

So today, I've stuck with my shaky ringmaster impersonation. I hop out there, introduce the act, and get out of the way.

Benvolio is lying on the ground, feet in the air like a possum playing dead, balancing a flaming baton on his calloused soles. I think it's pretty impressive, but the audience isn't biting. They have blank expressions, as if thinking about what they'll have for dinner later.

All eight of them.

• • • •

• • • •

"STEP RIGHT IN, LADIES and gentlemen, step right in! I promise, I vow, I guaran-ring-a-ding-tee that you all shall be thrilled out of your skulls tonight!"

I stand outside the colorful tent, my ringmaster's jacket fluttering in the crisp breeze. Gold patches are sewn on the shoulders, and a black top hat makes me just that much taller than the crowd swarming around me.

We've moved the tent across state lines for our first booking in years. Honestly, we could've taken the show on the road months ago, but I loved the fact that people were traveling from miles around to come see us. Make 'em work for it, I said. But it feels like the right time to expand our territory. Let people on the streets and highways see our trucks, let passersby in Connecticut spot our bright big-top from across town.

"Hurry in, hurry!" I flourish. "We're running out of seats, tickets are scarce! Soon enough, your chances to see our show will be...*extinct*!"

A few nearby people laugh at the joke, but most are too focused on getting inside to hear what I'm saying. It's a good joke, though—I'll use that one later.

Janelle maneuvers her way through the maze of people and ends up beside me. "Wow..." she breathes, a dazed smile splitting her cheeks. She doesn't have the clipboard tonight.

"I know," I lean in to say to her, "look at this crowd!"

"Well, that too." She elbows me in the ribs. "But I was talking about you, hooch. You've taken to the showman role pretty good. Seems like yesterday you were writing the show order on your hand."

I beam and gesture to the sea of people rushing into the tent. "When the water rises, the boat rises with it."

Janelle cackles and salutes. "Aye-aye, captain!"

I can't count all the customers. They aren't even waiting patiently in line—they're knocking each other out of the way, buzzing like bees, excited to see what we have inside.

"Come on in, folks! Welcome to Townshend's Festival of Time! Get ready to see things no human eye has seen this side of the calendar! We only have a few seats left. Better get a move on!"

• • • •

• • • •

I LOVE TO READ. ANYTHING I can get my hands on simply transports me. Well, anything except for newspapers. I'm not one for current events. But mysteries, encyclopedias, sciences, histories, romances... Books are my window to another world.

I'm walking through Hartsdale to the public library—if I was ever charged with murder and the cops were looking for me, folks would say, "Stake out the library. He'll show up soon."

Janelle is right beside me. She's a bit taller than me, her stringy hair making it so that I've never gotten a full view of her face. But she's smart and kind and really knows how things ought to go.

Right now, however, I wish she wasn't right.

"We're circling the drain, Nico." Her shoes clap on the sidewalk.

"We've circled before." I ball my hands into fists and blow on them. The winter is killer this year. "It'll perk up once it thaws, like usual."

"Nico, it's more serious than that. If we don't hit our goal within two weeks, we're done."

I gulp but continue my stride. I can't react like any other 24-year-old—I'm in charge of this circus, these people's jobs. "Okay, what's the goal?"

"A number without a negative sign in front of it."

"Loud and clear." I give her a sad smile. "See you in a bit for the night show."

We part ways, me turning to walk up the stone stairs into the library as Janelle goes on with her day. It strikes me that I don't know all that much about her.

I enter the building, my shoes made of iron. I rub my eyes until fireworks explode across my vision, but that does nothing to alleviate the monster headache setting up shop.

I nod to Wanda the librarian and begin to wander through the book-lined aisles. The aroma of well-used pages floats past me.

What can I do? Honestly, what? I'm no business wizard. I'm not an entertainer. Coastal millionaires and titans of industry have lost their jobs, their careers, their legacies. The whole country is hurting. What chance does a dingy circus just outside of New York City have?

Maybe I need to let Townshend's Shanty fade out. Take it behind the barn and shoot. Let the handful of employees move on and find new paths.

It hurts my heart to even think it. But maybe.

My feet pad across the decades-old carpet, unconsciously taking me to the history section. I just want something to distract me until I have to head back to the tent. A dark book spine looks at me from eye-level: *Anatomy of an Excavation*. The discovery of King Tut's tomb. I remember hearing about that when I was younger, back when the news wasn't always disheartening.

Sounds pretty interesting. I take the book, check out with Wanda, and reenter the cold day.

The sun is gray behind a blanket of clouds. Should've brought my jacket. Then I remember the only jacket I own is the ringmaster one that makes me look like an escaped loony. I chuckle without humor at the thought of me walking around town wearing that thing.

The route I walk is second nature to me by now. I wind through the neighborhoods and little shops of Hartsdale until the human constructions are overtaken by trees. I trade mailboxes for bushes, asphalt for grass, and chitchat for bird chirps.

Sprain Point Park is so peaceful and personal. There are places for kids to play and old people to play checkers, but that's only a sliver of the whole area. The rest is untamed forest, and people rarely venture into that part. So that's where I go. Taking a breath among the foliage is like sipping from a mountain stream. Even this far into winter, the leaves are green and bold, challenging the cold to do its worst.

There's no better place to relax, read, and listen to your own thoughts.

I leave the designated path and hike over the roots for a while. From way down here, the trees look like the legs of giants—centuries-old giants, unmoved by worries about jobs or the government or Wall Street. I'm jealous.

No matter how hard I strain my ears, I don't hear a human voice, no footfalls other than my own. This is the life.

I scan for a nice sitting spot, somewhere mossy and comfortable, out of the breeze. Not too many rocks or twigs or intruding roots.

No luck so far. I keep walking.

With each step, something in the distance becomes more and more visible. At first, I think it's just my eyes being tricky, but nope. As I move, its shape and color become more distinct. I'm not sure what it is, but it's big and metal and doesn't belong here in the park.

My steps hesitate for a moment...but it's definitely inanimate, so I keep moving.

About twenty feet long, purple paint chipping off, rusted on the corners and edges... It's an old bus. One of those big passenger beasts that you can ride from Portland to Portland. The door is missing, the windows are cracked and foggy, and the whole thing sits on three flat tires. Weeds have sprouted from the ground and wrapped themselves around the wheels as if trying to prevent it from escaping.

I slide a hand across its metal hull, cold to the touch. The name of the company is carved on its side: "*Cronos Bus Lines.*" Never heard of it. I look all around me. The trees are thick and bunched together, Mother Nature acting as their only gardener. No tiretracks at all, not even faded ones. The bus can't fit between the trees, much less drive on the uneven ground.

And I don't want to think about the fact that I've explored these woods for years and never seen this thing.

How in the world did it get here?

A chill runs down my bones, but it quickly passes. After all, it's just a bus. Harmless.

The breeze picks up again and I remember how much I hate not having a jacket. A wheezy whistle comes from inside the bus. My heart rate peaks until I realize it's only the wind sliding through the broken windows. Why am I so jumpy?

I peer through the open maw where a door used to be. Three short stairs lead into the metal beast. The driver's seat is tattered but still plush. A bit dirty but not stained or gross.

In I go. One foot on a step, as if testing the waters, then the other.

All the passengers' seats have grown a new skin of moss and grime. A few sprigs of stuffing peek out of the leather coverings, but otherwise, the interior's condition could be way worse. There's a booth with a closed door at the back—a lavatory would be my guess.

I sit where the driver would, and dust explodes around me. The sunlight is muted and brown, but the place is surprisingly comfortable. It's like my own private reading nook. No one can bother me here.

The King Tut book moves out from under my arm and onto my lap. I check the table of contents and flip to the chapter about what they found inside the boy pharaoh's tomb. An ancient board game called Senet, scarab pendants, chariots, weapons...

I fixate on the paragraph about what they call "canopic jars." Haven't heard of anything like this. Apparently, the Egyptians would remove the organs from dead bodies that were about to be turned into mummies. They believed royalty would need their heart and lungs and everything in the afterlife—for what, who knows. But they'd put each organ in a clay jar, and then, they put all the jars in a huge shrine. There was a jar for Tut's stomach, liver—

Thunk.

The sound comes from the back of the bus. I jolt to my feet, the book clattering to the floor, and I spin around. I call out, "Hey!" The word ricochets a dozen times down the length of the metal bus.

A breeze rocks the floor beneath my feet, but there's no other sound, no movement except for the swaying branches on the other side of the spider-webbed windows.

I think it came from inside the lav.

Inch by inch, I move down the aisle, crunching dead leaves and clumps of soil. The door looms larger as I approach.

Still no sound.

I reach out and swiftly rip open the lavatory door. It swings without a squeak or a hitch.

Black walls. Tin floor. Spotless. Not a speck of dust. It's a tiny room, and the air is very heavy, like I'm inside an army tank. The only thing I see is...

Sitting on the floor. About the size of a bottle of wine. A jar. Its top is shaped like the head of a pharaoh. Like the head of the jar I'd seen a picture of in the book I'd dropped by the driver's seat.

I tremble as I bend down and pick up the jar. It's covered in dirt and dust, as if I'd just dug it out of the ground. I'm no geologist, but it feels like clay.

I desperately want to open the lid and see what's inside. But I don't dare.

What just happened?

• • • •

• • • •

IT FINISHES FEASTING on Janelle in a matter of seconds.

I feel like I've been shoved in the chest, and I fall onto my back. The dark sky stares down at me, not a star in sight.

This is my doing. I brought this thing here. Every death, every drop of blood, it's all on me.

I scramble to my feet and run into the maze of parked cars. I need to get as many obstacles between myself and the creature as possible.

My lungs pulse in my chest, burning as I pull in the frigid night air and breathe out puffs of smoke. The ringmaster's coat flaps against my legs, but I'd lost the cheap top hat in the chaos inside the tent. I'm no master of ceremonies anymore—I'm just a scared, stupid kid.

I hear something over my pounding heartbeat. Galloping. Snarling. Otherworldly humming.

I peek over my shoulder and scream. It's right behind me, giving chase, ready for seconds. It roars, and its breath is even colder than the winter air.

My legs turn to spaghetti, and I crash to the ground. Every nerve in my body braces itself as I slide against a parked car. I inhale and hold my breath, too petrified to move.

It plants its four feet right in front of me and leans in, like a curious hound. It has no eyes or face, just a long, slender snout that I know can open up and reveal horrific teeth. Its legs end in nubs, no toes or claws.

I don't move. Can't move. Don't breathe.

The creature hovers over me for a moment that feels like an eternity. My hands are numb, and my lungs are about to pop like balloons. But I don't budge.

It snorts, sounding...disappointed? No, that can't be. But it sulks away, moving back to the tent. Back where it knows there's more food.

I wait. I wait for it to be fifty yards away. No, a hundred yards. Then I exhale and inhale at the same time, drinking fresh air. Tears I didn't know I'd shed drip from my chin.

For some reason, it hadn't attacked me. I was ripe for the picking, and it'd left me alone.

I grab the car's side-mirror and lift myself up, my arms and legs as limp as those of a marionette. I look back toward the Townshend's tent, and what I see is straight out of a nightmare.

People are running in every direction, some bloodied, all pale and shrieking. The creature chases them with glee, as if I'd brought it to a first-class game reserve. Its legs are long and slender as it runs. A greyhound from Hell.

A man in an overcoat runs past an elderly woman helping a boy. The woman can barely stand, quivering either from terror or the cold—likely both—but she has stopped to grab the boy's hand anyway. The boy looks up at the woman with wide eyes like she's a guardian angel.

The man in the coat reels up a leg and kicks the back of the woman's knee. She tumbles to the ground, bringing the boy down with her.

In an instant, the Hellhound is on top of them both, sensing downed prey.

And the man in the coat gets away.

Better them than me, I bet he's thinking.

I want to vomit. I want to scream until my throat is raw.

One of the tipped-over floodlights ignites the dead grass directly under its powerful beam. With so much dry tinder, the flickers quickly turn into a blaze, greedily spreading across the field. Black smoke billows into the air with ravenous vigor.

The Hellhound stops its prowl and turns to the flames, head raised, snout twitching. It sprints across the field and leaps into the fire, snapping at the smoke and smashing the floodlight.

I lean against the car and collect my thoughts.

Can it be?

It has no sight. It chased after me but then walked right past me once I stopped breathing. And now, it charges straight at the smoke.

I rifle through the catalog of all the books I've read in Sprain Point Park over the years.

This...this *thing* came from another realm outside of ours. One without our natural laws. It's not accustomed to sound, has no need for sight.

It reacted to the fire, but ignored me because I wasn't breathing.

CO_2. Carbon dioxide. That's what it picks up on, how it gets around.

That's it. That's how I can lure it away from the people.

Oh God, I hope that's it.

• • • •

DECEMBER 15, 1933
Hartsdale, NY
_9:25 a.m._

• • • •

JANELLE BURSTS INTO the tent. "Nico, they said yes!"

I bolt up from my seat. In the past, during downtime before and after shows, I would've had to sit in the stands where audience members leave their peanut shells and tissues. But now, times are good enough for me to spring for a nice reclining chair. It's like I'm lounging in Olympus.

A smile explodes across my face. "Honestly?"

She doesn't have to elaborate. I know exactly what she's talking about—the only thing that's been on our minds the past week.

Our neighboring city of Yonkers wants us to perform at its New Year's Eve festival. It may not be NYC, but it definitely isn't Hartsdale. We'd be right up there with successful bands, comics, celebrities... Our name on a marquee, raking in more money than I've ever seen in my life.

I can't believe it.

"Honestly." Janelle quivers and claps. "I never thought I'd see the day!"

We cheer and embrace. I've always considered Janelle a good friend, but the past few months have made us practically inseparable. Except when I slip away to the park, of course.

The two of us pull apart, our happiness echoing in the tent. She lets out a delighted sigh and says, "You better go all-out for this one."

"Definitely!" I begin to pace, excitement thumping in my chest, my gut. "I think we could combine all of our lineups into one! Benvolio will open, warm the crowd up. We pass out popcorn, peanuts, cider, and hot chocolate. Then we trot out all of our previous hits, one after the other."

"No, Nico, I'm talking something brand new. Something no one's ever seen before."

I pause. I've gone too far before, and there've been consequences—of course, no one but me knows that. "Well... We've been successful before. It may not be smart to push our luck in such a big venue."

"I gotta disagree," she presses. "We'll be on the biggest stage outside of Manhattan, being seen by people from all over the region, with folks hearing about us for the very first time. That's *exactly* when to go all-in! Hit 'em with a haymaker and make 'em regret never seeing us before!"

A beat of quiet. I remember a book I've passed by in the library countless times, too scared to pick it up, too cowardly to act. The black book with a chilling, tempting title.

"I'll see what I can come up with."

• • • •

• • • •

I SLEEPWALK THROUGH the day's matinee show—I'm sure the single-digit audience doesn't mind—and sprint to the library as soon as I can. Janelle's eyes drill holes in my back as I run out of the tent, but I do my best to ignore her. This is important.

Wanda waves to me as I storm in, and I nod back. It feels like I'm in a controlled frenzy, a merry-go-round on its highest setting. I move through the shelves and grab random books, barely looking at the titles.

"My, my," Wanda coos when I slam the stack down on the counter. "Someone's got a literary appetite today!" She grabs her due-date stamp and holds it aloft, like a cowboy getting ready for a showdown.

Seconds tick by at a glacial pace as she flips open each of the ten books, stamps their inside covers, and sets them aside. All I can think about is getting back to that faded purple bus in the woods.

I stuff the checked-out books in a bag, sling them over my shoulder, and chart a course for the middle of Sprain Point Park. As I hike over the roots and twigs, I expect to find nothing. No bus, no clay jar, just bushes and squirrels and a heaping dose of embarrassment. It'd certainly be unnerving to realize I dreamt the whole thing up, but not nearly as unnerving as the alternative.

But I follow the unmarked path I took yesterday, and there it is. Big, purple, wrapped in weeds, proudly branded "*Cronos.*"

So. It's not some fever-induced mirage. Good to know.

I move to one tree in particular and rummage through the leaves at its base. My fingers clink against something hard, and I remove the casket-shaped jar. As real as ever.

I'd stayed up all night reading and rereading and re-rereading the section about the canopic jars in my King Tut book. No photos accompany the text, but based on the detailed descriptions, this is one of them. I don't know how or why, but this is a jar from the pharaoh's tomb, containing one of his mummified organs.

I rise and meander over to the bus, carefully clutching the jar with both hands. I set it on the dented hood so I can keep an eye on it while I'm in the driver's seat.

Up the few steps, into the metal belly. Back in the plush seat. My gaze flits out the foggy windshield—it's still there, Tut's tiny painted eyes staring back at me.

I plop down my bag of books and rummage through it. What did I even get? I was in such a daze, I barely paid attention.

Ooh. *Treasure Island* by Robert Stevenson. I look back at the lavatory door for just a second, and my palms start to sweat.

I settle deeper into the seat and flip through the novel's pages. I've read this one before, so I know right where I'm going. The scene where Jim and Long John Silver find the fabled treasure.

Stacks of gold in a cave. Heaps of coins, mountains of jewels, glittering, dazzling, worth a thousand fortunes.

I take a deep breath and read through it one more time. Then I tumble out of the seat and run to the lav door. Rip it open.

Nothing. Just a cold puff of air.

Hmm. I slump back to the front of the bus, rubbing my eyes. The lack of sleep is catching up to me in a hurry. I flop in the driver's seat, glance out the windshield, and bolt upright.

The clay jar is shimmering, as if I'm looking at it from far away in the scorching sun. It's there, then it's not, then it's back. The solid object is flickering in and out right in front of me.

Treasure Island clatters to the floor. I exit the bus too quickly, tripping over my feet and missing the stairs entirely. I scrape my knees on the mossy ground, but I barely notice. I leap to the hood and grab Tut's jar, but it's unlike anything I've felt before. It's like I'm holding water cupped in both hands—mushy, slipping away, held together by the thinnest of strands.

And it's gone. My hands are empty. I can still feel the clay against my skin, like the residual stinging after being slapped. But it's not here anymore.

Some instinct tells me to check my watch.

It's been exactly 24 hours since I found the jar on the bus.

Okay...

I reach into the bus, grab the King Tut book, and open it. The leaves high above me cast deformed shadows across the white pages. The book's bent spine flips to the exact spot I was looking for, the same paragraph I'd pored over the night before.

And right there, at the bottom on the page, practically a footnote, is a sentence that wasn't there before.

My heart booms like a bass drum. *Are you sure?* I ask myself, but I interrupt my internal questioning—*Yeah, I'm sure. I've stared at this page for hours.*

I whisper the new sentence to the silent woods: "Strangely, the tomb's shrine did not contain the canopic jar holding the young king's liver. This is most unusual, considering Egyptian burial practices, but the jar was simply nowhere to be found."

I know where that jar is.

Or where it *was*, I guess.

It was here, in Sprain Point Park, New York, 1933. In my hands.

Now it's gone. Erased from history. Forever.

I lean against the bus before I collapse.

How can this be? What hole in the universe have I stumbled across?

One more thought crosses my mind. Like a soldier in a foxhole about to charge, I steady myself and return to the driver's seat.

I dig through the bag and pull out a thick, dusty volume: a biography of Benjamin Franklin. I open the book on my lap and read.

One blustery afternoon, Franklin had constructed a kite out of a white handkerchief and two strings, one of hemp, the other of silk. To this kite, he attached—

Thunk.

My heart twitches. Yes.

I leave the seat and approach the lav door once again. Before, I was scared, suspicious of what was inside. Now, I'm a conqueror.

The noiseless hinges give way. Sitting on the floor is just what I'd imagined: a white hankie fashioned into a kite, two strings dangling below, and a brass key.

I kneel down and reach out. The fabric is still wet from the Philadelphia thunderstorm in 1752. I touch the key and get a static shock.

A laugh explodes from my throat.

I stand and close the door, scared that I might get too attached to the kite. Best to put it out of sight as quickly as possible. As soon as the doorknob clicks into place, I feel the metal frame pulse a little bit. Like the cosmos taking a breath.

When I open it again, the kite's gone. The floor isn't even damp.

I sit in the back row of passenger's seats because I don't think my legs would support me all the way to the front of the bus. I lean my forehead against the cold metal frame and try to order my thoughts.

So.

I can summon things from the past. But only when sitting in that driver's seat and visualizing them perfectly—maybe reading about them merely helps, maybe the books are a key ingredient to this whole thing. I don't know.

I can't create fictional things, like Long John Silver's gold. Only real objects.

The things I bring here can only stay out of their time for 24 hours. Otherwise, they crumble. And all of history is rewritten.

Wow.

My mind reels with the possibilities. It's like I'm looking down an infinite hallway filled with locked doors, and I was just handed the master key.

Maybe I could bring up some of that treasure from King Tut's tomb I'd read about. We'd divvy it up amongst the Townshend employees, and none of us would ever have to work again. We'd be free to enjoy life, indulge our passions, explore the world—

Wait. I calm my galloping imagination.

This isn't a genie that can conjure something out of nothing. It's a grocery store. Every dollar I take out of this bus already exists somewhere else. It'd be mighty suspicious for me to try to buy a house with King Tut's gilded fan, and the last thing I want is to be arrested as an Egyptian grave-robber, despite having never left the Atlantic Northeast.

Whatever I bring here, I have to send back. I don't want to tear history apart at the seams—I'm just a kid trying to keep a circus above water.

But maybe...

I smile.

Townshend's Shanty might have a couple new exhibits tomorrow.

• • • •

JANUARY 5, 1933
Hartsdale, NY
12:08 p.m.

• • • •

I NEED TO BE CAREFUL. Oh so careful. I don't want anyone to get hurt, and I don't want to accidentally make it so that wheels are never invented, or something insane like that.

So today, I've brought a piece to reel people in, maybe tell their friends about.

A few minutes before the show is set to start, I pull Janelle aside and speak to her quietly. "Listen, I have something I want to try."

She looks at me, surprised—as much as I've endeavored to help the circus, I've never been outgoing or creative enough to roll out a new act. "Okay, then. You chose until right before showtime to tell me." Not a question, just a droll observation. "Care to share?"

"It's..." How do I even begin to explain? "I made a contact that can really help us out, get some interesting stuff. You have to trust me."

Janelle opens to her mouth to protest, but she thinks for a moment, then cranes her neck to peek at the audience. From my angle, I can't see how many we have, but she looks at me and shrugs. "Go for it."

Must be a tiny crowd.

A few minutes later, I burst onto the stage. Very unlike me—I usually take several deep breaths and have to work up the courage. Now, I'm charging out, guns blazing. I think it's so I don't have time to talk myself out of it.

"Hello, hello, everyone!" I wave with one hand and hold something with the other: a long, slender object wrapped in a blanket.

Janelle's face was right earlier. We have six people in the crowd.

Here goes nothing.

"You all came here on the right day." I wipe a bead of sweat from my lip with a shaky finger. But I don't stop. "I just came into possession of something wondrous. Something Townshend's Shanty has never seen before."

I gulp, trying to banish my nerves to someplace I can't feel their influence. A couple of audience members have leaned forward, listening intently. Now that's something *I've* never seen before.

"Journey with me, if you will, to the mysterious land of Africa. Deep in the unknown, one man creates order out of madness, a kingdom out of nothing!" Wow. I'm getting pretty good at this. "This warrior wields a weapon with lethal skill, and all who challenge him fall. I give you..." I unwrap the blanket and hold the historical treasure high above my head. "The spear of Shaka Zulu!"

I yell louder than I mean to, but it bursts from my gut—I can't help it.

The spear I hold is about three feet long, shorter than most, and its blade is almost as broad as a sword's. The wooden handle is coarse in my hands. It's a truly fearsome thing, and even as I hold it, I tremble for two reasons. One: It looks like it could slice and dice me if I blink at it wrong. And two: Shaka Zulu himself honestly used it 200 years ago. In fact, I see a fleck of dried blood on its point, and it strikes me... Shaka Zulu used this very spear *yesterday*.

My knees almost buckle.

I can't say the same for the audience. I realize I've been standing center-stage for about ten seconds, grinning up at the spear like a loony.

No reaction.

I lower the spear and feel my face getting red. "So i-it's something, huh?"

One of the men in the bleachers says, "It's a stick."

"Well," I sputter, "well, yeah, I suppose. But this is the real thing. The real spear."

The man waggles his eyebrows. "Mhmm. Sure it is."

I scan the expressions of the rest of the crowd members. They all seem to be on the same page. This is just a branch some poor broke circus boy taped to a pocketknife and is calling an artifact.

A fake, they think.

I swallow my shame, grab the blanket off the floor, and scuttle offstage.

Janelle sighs and puts a kind hand on my shoulder. "No real harm done, Nico."

But I've already made up my mind.

They want something big. Something undeniably real.

If that's what they want—I adjust my ringmaster's jacket—that's exactly what they'll get next time.

• • • •

• • • •

ONE DAY, A HUGE IDEA hits me. I start bringing in famous garments, and I advertise like a madman.

Try on Marie Antoinette's wigs and dresses! Wear Julius Caesar's robes! Take a walk in Emperor Huang's slippers! Napoleon's medals, Lincoln's stovepipe hat, Montezuma's headdress, and the most popular ticket... Charles II's breathtaking, elaborate crown, gold shining and jewels sparkling in the sunlight.

The crowds eat it up. We start making more money than we know what to do with.

I'm always extremely careful to get these items from the bus early in the morning and return them late at night. Not only am I completely alone in the dark woods, safe from wandering eyes, but I have a huge buffer of time before the 24-hour-deadline. There's no way I can let these things fade away like Tut's liver did.

This strategy also helps with my sales pitch. "One day only, folks! Try on a Union uniform, still smelling like the gunpowder of Antietam! Hurry, hurry, hurry—you only have a few hours left to wield the scepter of Catherine the Great!"

I have a huge assortment of historical fashion for people to try—one day and one day only—and then we take a break for a few weeks, letting our usual circus acts shine. Build up anticipation, let word of mouth travel all over the region. I also take this time to do plenty of research in the library before choosing my next attraction and taking those books to the Cronos bus. This ensures that I have new items when people come back.

No one will ever see the same thing twice, I promise the audience...and myself. No one will ever get bored at Townshend's.

• • • •

• • • •

"JANELLE, I'M TRYING again."

"Nico..." She chooses her words carefully, not wanting to hurt me. "It didn't go so well last time."

"I know. Believe me, I know. But that's why I've waited so long."

After the Zulu spear disaster, I'd wanted to try again the next day—that very night, actually—but I didn't. I'd realized I'd rushed into things without sketching out a plan first. So for the next couple weeks, I did a lot of reading, a lot of thinking, and a lot of dreaming.

"I'm ready tonight. And it's gonna work." No room for negotiation.

The secret pocket in my jacket shifts a bit. What's inside wants to get out.

I clear my throat and jaunt out to greet the audience. About fifteen people. A typical night crowd. But this isn't a typical night. It will never be typical around here ever again.

"Ladies and gentlemen..." My voice quivers, but not from shame or stage-fright. Not in the least. I can't wait to unleash what I have in store.

"I'm so glad each and every one of you is here. What we have to offer you is something no eye has beheld in the history of *Homo sapiens*. I..." No words can capture what I'm feeling, so I just chuckle. "You're gonna love this. I now ask that the tent's exit flap be firmly tied."

The audience murmurs as a few employees secure the big-top's only entrance and exit. The employees murmur too. They're just as confused as the crowd. I love it.

I steal a side-glance and see Janelle offstage, wringing her hands, watching, waiting for me to crash again.

Not gonna happen. I give her a wink and a nod.

"Everyone," I reach into my jacket, "meet the past."

I release the latch on a hidden compartment, opening the little door. As if by magic, a dozen wisps of cloud zip out of my sleeves and flutter all around the tent. They bounce off the walls, ruffle people's hair, and circle over us.

Then the sounds reach our ears. They're so high-pitched and modest, people in the crowd have to shush their neighbors. Only once everyone's quiet do we hear...

Tweet. Tweet.

"These," I say in a hushed voice, forcing everyone to lean in, "are the archaeopteryx. But I've taken to calling them Tufts."

I like my name for them. They aren't wisps of cloud at all, but tiny birds, each about the size of a silver dollar. The crowd stares up, smiling. Ah, what smiles.

"Take a good look, ladies and gents. You are the first to ever interact with these precious birds...other than myself, of course. The archaeopteryx went extinct nearly fifty million years ago."

Their whimsical smiles turn to skeptical glares real quick.

"Shocking, I know. But take a good look. Janelle," I quietly call over my shoulder, "could you please grab the bags of fruit and pass one to each person?"

Janelle does so. As she walks by me, she offers a glance that's equal parts amazement and suspicion. I expected nothing less from her.

"Now," I say once all fifteen people have a paper bag of blackberries, "stay very, very, *very* still. There's no reason to be scared."

"S-So they don't eat meat?" one of the patrons asks, eyes wider than silver dollars.

"Oh, they're carnivores," I respond with a rakish smile. "But tiny little birds won't eat a person." I wait a beat. "Probably."

The nervous energy sharpens into tangible fear...just as I intended. This was a gamble, but it's paying off. No one has left the tent. They want to be a part of this. The hint of danger has glued them to their seats.

"Stay still," I repeat quietly. "They're small and jittery. Let 'em come to you."

There isn't a sound in the entire tent except for the frail flapping of tiny wings and the occasional chirp. Everyone in the bleachers sits like a statue, looking up, hoping a prehistoric bird will pick them. The mere fact that they're going along with this premise is a win in my book. But I want a home-run.

Flap. Tweet. Flap.

A minute passes.

Tweet.

One bird breaks formation and darts onto a teenaged girl's shoulder. She purses her lips to keep from squealing. It'd be a joyful squeal, I can tell. She elbows her boyfriend and points at the bird, silently saying, "*Get a load of this, Gary!*" Or something like that.

Soon, all of the birds have flitted down and landed amongst the audience. They peck at the berries, their bright black eyes staring up at the *Homo sapiens*.

Pointy beaks. Bat-like wings. Tiny bodies that look like they'd disintegrate in the wind.

No one has ever seen a bird like this before.

I can tell by their faces, gasps, and whispers. I've got them.

"From the smallest of small," I say, increasing my volume with every word, "to the next in line!" I flourish, and the people are left speechless.

From stage-right comes a bird as big as an ostrich, walking on scaly legs and huge, monstrous feet. Its body is covered in feathers as black and greasy as crude oil, and although its wings are folded to its side, you can tell they're enormous. Its gray neck is several feet long, allowing its fluffy head to look down on the crowd. Bright red eyes and an orange beak point at each person, one by one.

Any sliver of doubt the audience held in reserve has evaporated. No one on any continent at any time has seen a creature like *this*. They don't know how, but this kid in an ill-fitting jacket is parading around with prehistoric animals.

"Meet the Eastern Moa, visiting from the Pleistocene epoch. Cute, huh?"

I know he's a leaf-eater. But I don't tell the audience that.

The giant prehistoric bird stops center-stage, unfurls its wings, and lets out a seismic caw. Everyone covers their ears, and the tiny wispy birds take flight in a tizzy.

"Ladies and gentlemen, you all came on a very special night." I pace across the stage, relishing the power I hold over man and beast at this moment. The Eastern Moa curls up on the ground at my feet, and the crowd stares, mesmerized.

"From now on, we're going to be doing things a little differently around here. Your old favorites aren't going anywhere, but we're upping the ante. Benvolio the strongman won't just be twirling batons and ripping Yellow Pages. He'll lift dinosaur femurs and tame sabertooth tigers! The past is here to stay, everyone. Tell your friends, tell your folks, and when they don't believe you, bring 'em to our next show. Welcome..."

I spread my arms, and the tiny birds swirl around me, drawn to the berries hidden in my coat. They all flutter into the secret compartment, gone in a flash. I lower my arms and close the hidden cage, the birds having seemingly vanished. The crowd gapes. I feel like I'm floating.

"...to Townshend's Festival of Time."

• • • •

• • • •

MY HEART FEELS LIKE it's about to burst through my chest. Even though the air is ice-cold, sweat beads my forehead, my palms, my everywhere.

I can't do this. I don't even know how or where to start.

All I have is a shaky, homemade theory that the Hellhound "sees" by smelling carbon dioxide. So what?

Earlier that day, when we'd set up the big-top tent for the New Year's show in Yonkers, I'd made sure our location was right on the edge of Sprain Point Park. That way, it'd be easy and inconspicuous when me and my hired-hands brought the creature into the tent before showtime.

Thank the big guy above. We wouldn't stand a chance if the Cronos bus wasn't nearby.

Maybe...

I force myself to think, but it's like running through wet sand.

Maybe we can wait it out. Get everyone to safety, call in the cops and the army, keep our distance as the creature runs amok. Then, once the 24-hour limit has run out, it'll crumble into nothingness.

Even as I think this through, I know it's not an option. The Hellhound is too dangerous. It ravaged the entire crowd in a matter of minutes. Maybe eventually, if they get enough guns on it, the army could take it out, but that'd be hours from now. The creature could rip the entire city to shreds if it wanted. The handful of deaths it has already inflicted is sickening enough.

No, I have to get it into the bus's lavatory, send it back to the pit it came from.

But how to do that, how to do that...

How can I lure it into the woods? What produces carbon dioxide? My breath? Yeah, but that's not enough. A car? True, but I can't drive between the trees.

The trees.

I dash into the tent, grab Benvolio's baton, and leave before the stench of blood overwhelms me. A flick of a match later, the baton is ablaze. I run into the woods, headed toward the bus.

Every twenty feet or so, I reach out my arm and smack a branch with the torch. After a minute of breathless sprinting, I peek over my shoulder.

A path of smoke and flame is now cutting through Sprain Point Park, a deadly trail of breadcrumbs for the Hellhound to follow. Straight to me.

I keep running.

• • • •

• • • •

"MY, MY, IF I GAVE YOU a quarter for every book you've checked out, Nico, you could buy the Chrysler Building."

I drop a pile of hardcovers onto the checkout desk, flecks of dust and old glue poofing out like smoke in a volcanic eruption. I smile as Wanda begins her long, arduous task of stamping each cover, and I halfway engage in her small talk. But I'm too excited about tonight to pay that much attention.

Me and my hired-hands already took it from the bus early this morning, and it's waiting in a pen at the tent. Judging by their faces, tonight's show is gonna be a good one.

A couple months ago, I wised up. I'm no strongman, and I only have two hands. If I'm gonna keep upping the ante—which I want and have to do—I'm gonna need some help. So once we had some money to spend, I went into Manhattan and hired a few biceps with men attached to them. They don't know about the books and the time travel and all that, and they're paid well to not ask questions. They just help me carry and/or wrangle our exhibits out of the bus, to the tent, and back to the bus.

Day in, day out. It's always exciting for them, and it allows me to bring so much more than I ever could by myself.

For our more surly, sentient exhibits, I've given them metal batons. They're also armed with guns, but I made it very clear: Violence is only to be used as an absolute last resort, and they're only to shoot at the ground right in front of the creature. Under no circumstances are they to fire upon anything that comes out of the bus. Usually, the animals are fairly compliant—more confused and scared than aggressive—and loud noises tend to make them obedient. We've had no injuries so far.

Wanda's voice raises, indicating that she asked a question. Her wide, smiling eyes look up at me.

I'm not listening, but I laugh and nod.

Must be sufficient. She giggles and says, "Oh, that's just great!"

The universe taps me on the shoulder.

No. I need to stop blaming this on some faceless energy. It's me—it's my own pride, brain, and gut tapping me on the shoulder.

Still, I turn my head, and my eyes immediately find the spine of the book with the black cover. For months, I've been tempted to try it out. See what lives in its pages. Surely it would sell tons and tons of tickets at the tent.

But no. It's too...something. I don't even know if it's dangerous, but the uncertainty is precarious enough. I'll stick with the past.

For now.

Wanda finishes her stamping, and I tuck the stack under my arm and leave before the black book can tempt me again. It whispers its title to me as I push open the library door: *Theories on Parallel Realities.*

• • • •

• • • •

THE CROWD ROARS WITH applause. I join them as a tap-dancing troupe dressed in the Founding Fathers' authentic garb move offstage.

"Give it up for the Revolutionary Rockettes! Better than anything they have in the City, am I right, folks? Let me hear how much you love 'em!"

And the cheers get even louder. They course through my veins and make my breath shaky.

I'm constantly amazed at how compliant the masses are when they're told something with confidence. I've let people fire George Washington's musket and put their smudgy fingers all over Alexander the Great's armor—all without a word from the police, foreign or domestic. On a daily basis, I flaunt birds, reptiles, and plants that are scientifically extinct...but I do it with style, so it's okay.

Every single day, people stop me outside the tent and ask something along the lines of "Where do these amazing creatures come from?"

I always smile and say, "They took the bus!"

Everyone laughs. No one presses me for a real answer. They pay me, have their fun, and walk away with memories that'll last a lifetime.

As long as the people are smiling and clapping, I'm untouchable.

"And now, ladies and gentlemen..." I spread my arms. Silence swallows us all.

I'm unbelievably excited for this one. Ever since that day in January when I found the purple bus, I've wanted to bring out two things.

The first is a wooly mammoth. The size, the fur, the eyes, the trunk... What a crowd-pleaser that would be. But logistics have always gotten in the way. Mammoths are, obviously, way bigger than a bus-bound water closet. I have no idea how that would work—would the creature burst out of the lav, completely crushing the bus? Can't have that. And there's no way I'd bring a baby animal 10,000 years into the future. That just seems wrong.

The second creature is waiting backstage.

"After three hundred years in the dustpan of history, welcome back to the land of the living... The one, the only..." I spin and flourish. The spotlights converge on a squat ball of feathers that just waddled out. "The dodo!"

People go nuts, leaping to their feet to get a better view.

The beady eyes, the hawkish feet, the strange, circular beak. No one has ever seen this before.

The extinct bird looks at its rabid fans with curious indifference, preferring to itch under its wing.

• • • •

NOVEMBER 18, 1933
Greenwich, CT
9:53 p.m.

• • • •

"THANK YOU, LADIES AND gentlemen!" I wave to the crowd. "We are Townshend's Festival of Time. Tell your friends!"

Our first interstate performance is an undeniable triumph. We sold out of tickets, ran out of room in the stands, and shoved as many people into the tent as possible. We've made a fortune in food sales alone, but tonight, the money isn't what I'm focused on. The massive audience's reactions are worth more than gold. They cheered, gasped, rippled, murmured to each other, laughed, cried...

It couldn't possibly have gone any better.

Amid the deafening applause, I trot over to Janelle, who's hanging just off stage-right. I lean in and say, "Go outside and mingle in the crowd as they leave. Every tenth person, beckon them in real secretive. Tell them there's gonna be a special exhibit in the tent at eleven. Twelve dollars. It'll be worth it."

Janelle grins and nods. She doesn't question my vague directions anymore. "What's the exhibit, for when they ask?"

I tilt my hat off-balance so I look a bit impish. "Say they'll get the chance to hold a...terrible lizard."

An hour later, at 11:00 on the nose, I re-emerge onstage, wheeling a cage with a blanket over it. Waiting for me are dozens of people loitering around the tent—none of them are sitting, all rocking on their heels, tapping their toes, eager to see what I've brought them.

"So, so, so, welcome to the main show, everyone! I ask that you all form an orderly line in front of me, one in front of another, and show your exclusive ticket once you get to me."

One of the men in the crowd calls out, "What are we here for?" He's standing near a woman and five small kids, and I assume he wants to know what his eighty-plus dollars will get him.

I smile as if addressing a grumpy child. "Sir, tonight, you and all who are here will get up close and personal with..." I pull back the blanket, open the cage, and cradle the creature in my arms.

"Meet Lei."

Everyone is fixated on the small dinosaur I hold. Its marble eyes swivel around to take in its surroundings. The Lei is the size and weight of a duck, with very long tail feathers and sickle-like talons. It yawns, ruffling its gray feathers and revealing a single row of pinprick teeth on its lower jaw.

"This little guy is only known today because of one single fossil." I pet the dinosaur's head. "As far as humans know, this is the only Lei to ever exist. As rare as it gets."

No one breathes, no one moves. It feels like we're on holy ground.

"So who's first?"

· · · ·

NOVEMBER 19, 1933
  Greenwich, CT
  9:53 a.m.

. . . .

I DON'T BELIEVE IT.

We've made more money in one night than we did last month.

The special hands-on exhibit with the Lei was only supposed to last about an hour or two. But the line simply never ended. People must've bought another ticket from Janelle and looped through again. Or they told their friends, who told their friends, and the news spread like wildfire. One way or another, I stood in our big-top tent and passed the Lei dinosaur from person to person for the entire night.

My eyes are droopy and tingling, but I don't care. An electric thrill has stayed in the air all night long.

The Lei writhes in my arms, clawing at me, trying to get away, but I ignore its protests. "Next!"

I shove the creature into the arms of a little girl with blonde pigtails. Her eyes light up, and dimples as deep as the ocean form on her cheeks.

The Lei begins to bleat and sob, rubbing its head with one of its limp wings. I look closer...and I realize that, over the course of the night, its feathers have gone from gray to white.

The girl ignores the dinosaur's cries too. "Wow!" she exclaims. "Mama, look!"

Once her minute is up, she pouts and I take the Lei back. I rock it a bit, trying to comfort the small beast. "You'll be okay, little guy." I crane my neck. The line is still extended out the tent. "We're almost—"

Oh no. I look at my watch. 10:00.

It's almost been 24 hours.

I sprint out of the tent, my top hat clattering to the ground. I clutch the Lei to my chest as I shoulder my way through the crowd. The people boo, hiss, and scream curses at me, but I don't hear them.

But.

I realize too late. The tent isn't in Hartsdale today, near Sprain Point and the lavatory. We've crossed state lines into Connecticut. Miles and miles from the bus.

The small dinosaur whimpers in my arms and begins to shiver. It looks up at me with glassy eyes. And it begins to crumble.

Bit by bit. Just like Tut's clay jar.

No, not just like it—the jar was inanimate. This little guy is alive and terrified as it dissolves from reality, turns into mush, then into nothing. I'll remember its screams forever.

I fall to my knees in front of the big, colorful tent, the morning sunshine mocking me.

And as I sit there, crushed, a thought keeps stabbing at me.

That was the only Lei dinosaur to ever have been discovered. I stole it from its home before it was turned into a fossil.

It'll never be written about. The words I used to bring it here don't exist anymore.

• • • •

DECEMBER 31, 1933
 Hartsdale, NY
 6:15 a.m.

• • • •

I TAKE LONG STRIDES as I move through the woods. Big, confident steps. I have to look like I know what I'm doing. And mainly, I have to feel like it too.

My meaty hired-hands are with me. I've brought a couple extra guys to help with this new exhibit.

The black book is tucked under my arm. *Theories on Parallel Realities.* I skimmed through it at the library and found the paragraph I want to read while sitting in the driver's seat. Something about creatures from another plane of existence. A place with different natural laws.

Something no one has ever seen before. That's exactly what I want.

I need to grab this thing from the bus and get to Yonkers as quick as possible. We need to have the tent set up by noon, along with the concession booths, markers for parking, and all the other details.

Despite the chill, I wipe sweat from my lip.

"Remember," I say with all the authority I can muster, "don't shoot it. Fire at the ground. This thing is...different from all the others. It'll look strange. It'll be scared, so loud noises should do the trick. Don't mess around. As soon as I say so, get the chains and harnesses on it."

• • • •

• • • •

THAT CREATURE IS NOT of this world, and I was arrogant to bring it here.

I only stop sprinting when I'm in front of the bus. I stand there for a moment, panting, shivering. The flaming baton in my hand casts long, dancing shadows across the purple, metal monstrosity.

Heat sears the back of my neck. The trees are ablaze, and, thanks to the green leaves, the smoke is thick and smothering. A fiery maze leading straight to this amazing, terrible, wondrous, wicked bus.

Torch in hand, eyes set dead ahead, I climb the steps inside, just like I have so many times before. Now, however, I don't stop at the driver's seat—I go all the way to the door at the rear. I swing it open. Not a squeak or a hitch. And I step inside.

Making sure to leave the door open, I face outward. The bus stretches before me. It looks a mile long.

In a matter of seconds, the torch turns the air toxic. My eyes water, and ash coats the inside of my throat. But I don't mind. I deserve this.

It's getting hard to see. But I think I spy a flicker of movement at the front.

Yes. The creature climbs aboard, prowling like a lion. It points its head directly at me. I see a flash of teeth.

I don't have time to be terrified.

It charges, faster than the second-hand of a clock.

As it leaps onto me, I pull the lav door closed.

• • • •

???

. . . .

I FEEL LIKE I'M BEING pulled through a straw.

And now I'm here. Wherever here is.

I remember everything. Townshend's. Janelle. The library. The bus. The dodo and the Lei. The flaming baton. And it. The Hellhound.

I float in a sea of nothingness. Not blackness or darkness. Sheer nothing.

I hear a distant roar.

I was successful. I transported the Hellhound back from whence it came. Which is here. And I went with it.

And now here I am.

A place without light. Without time, without air.

A place with nothing but me.

And it.

Forever.

9

Wrong House

Freaky Factor: 3/3

CRUNCH, CLOMP. CRUNCH, clomp...

Rodney strode down the long country road, dirt and pebbles crying out in pain beneath his sneakers. He felt like he was marching into battle, with a bag full of supplies slung over his shoulder and a sense of purpose driving him forward.

As he walked, he sized up his target. At the far end of the road, barely the size of a Lego, was a lone farmhouse. In Rodney's sixteen years of life, he'd seen that house more times than he could remember. It'd been painted white decades ago, but now, only a few peeling flakes remained, like dandruff on a bald head. Huge willow trees surrounded the place, always swaying even in the smallest breeze.

But Rodney didn't know this house well because he'd visited it so many times. Just the opposite. His parents had pointed it out to him when he was little, telling him *not* to go there, to *never* step foot on that farm. As he got older, he and his friends always glared at the farmhouse as they passed by this long, lonesome road.

Why should he avoid this house? Because it belonged to Mr. Jeepers: the crankiest old man to have ever lived. He had no friends or family to speak of. His face had been hardened into a granite scowl by years of practice. He only talked to his neighbors by screaming at them to get off his property. And he never, ever handed out candy for Halloween.

Well, tonight was October 31st, and Rodney was in the mood for a few tricks, not treats.

He stopped at the edge of Jeepers's propertyline, then peered over his shoulder. "Ready?" he asked his little friends, Mason and Keith. Well, they weren't really his friends—they were more like his minions who did his bidding, and that was just how Rodney liked it.

They both nodded, eager to please the sixteen-year-old. Rodney had a driver's license and an extended curfew: two things the younger boys didn't have. They'd do just about anything to get Rodney to like them...and Rodney knew it. When he'd proposed this little Halloween excursion, they'd practically tripped over their shoelaces to agree.

They both held up their own bags of supplies. "Ready!"

"Let's teach this old man a lesson."

Rodney took a step onto the Jeepers farm. He'd expected the grass to sigh under his shoe, but instead, it also *crunch*ed, just like the country road. The lawn was dry and dead, having not been watered in what sounded like a million years. Rodney snorted—the old man wasn't much of a farmer if he couldn't even take care of his yard.

The two younger boys followed Rodney toward the house. The low branches of the willow trees surrounded them in a wispy hug. Rodney had never been so close to the house. The willow trees may have looked flowy and soft, but he felt like they were suffocating him. Like a pillow over his face.

He blinked heavily to refocus. He needed to get his head in the game. Mason and Keith were watching him.

Rodney set his hands on his hips and smiled mischievously. "Let's get to work."

The three boys chuckled as they unzipped their bags. They all pulled out rolls of toilet paper, which seemed to glow in the darkness.

The time had come to give Mr. Jeepers a TP'ing he'd never forget.

Rodney clutched a roll and cocked his arm back, ready to launch it up into a willow tree. But something caught his eye and made him pause. Up in the tree, a white figure was dangling from one of the branches.

"What the...?" Rodney narrowed his eyes to look closer.

It was a plastic skeleton, its legs and arms scraping together in the breeze. He turned on his heel, glancing around the property. Skeletons were strung up in all the trees. Just like the toilet paper, the plastic white bones stood out against the night.

Weird—Mr. Jeepers never decorated for Halloween.

"Uh...dude..." The sudden voice made Rodney jump, but it was only Mason. He'd also noticed the skeletons, and his eyes were round and jittery. "These things are creepy."

Rodney tried to still his pounding heart. "Let's... Let's do this quickly." He flicked his eyes between the hanging skeletons. "Okay, Mason, take the trees on the left side. Keith, you take the right. Got it?"

"Got it," said Mason.

And then, silence. Nothing but the creaking tree branches.

Rodney snarled. He wasn't in the mood for this. He snapped, "Keith! Where are you?" He spun in a circle, peering into the darkness for his little minion.

But Keith was nowhere to be found.

The grass crunched as Mason approached a low-hanging skeleton. With a shaky hand, he reached out and felt its bony leg. He pulled back as if he'd been burned. "I don't think these are plastic..."

"What are you talking—?"

THUMP. Something dropped to the ground. Judging by the sound, it was near where Mason had been standing.

Rodney ran over to see. Sitting on the dead grass was Mason's bag, tipped over, with TP spilling out. Rodney spun, but Mason was gone too.

"Nope. I'm out." With no one there to impress, Rodney dropped his roll of TP and sprinted away from the house.

The crunch of grass turned into the crunch of dirt. Rodney knew that if he could only get to the end of the road, with this freaky farmhouse far behind him, he'd be safe.

But a man stood in the middle of the road, blocking his path. Rodney screeched to a halt, frozen stiff in fear.

Mr. Jeepers glared at Rodney, a wicked glint in his eye. "Hello there." The old man's voice creaked like a wrought-iron gate.

"I-I-I..." Rodney forced the words past the bile in his throat. "I-I'm sorry I came onto your property, Mr. Jeepers." The apology tasted bitter on his tongue, but he'd say just about anything if it meant he could leave this place.

The old man didn't snarl. He didn't yell. He didn't even frown. Worse than all of that: He smiled. "No need to apologize, young man. Where are you going in such a hurry? Why don't you hang around for a while?"

Terror flooded Rodney's veins.

It looked like he'd TP'd the wrong house.

Costume Party

Freaky Factor: 3/3

MADDIE STOOD BEHIND the cash register at the costume shop, tapping a fingernail on the plastic countertop. Lost in her thoughts. Thinking about the night ahead. Tap. Tap. Tap...

Most people would be surprised that the costume shop was empty on the day of Halloween. But it made sense to Maddie—most people had planned ahead and gotten their costumes way in advance. In fact, the shelves were mostly empty. Other holidays had crazy rushes on the day of, but not Halloween.

Costumes, parties, large crowds, loud music... None of that appealed to Maddie. She was more of a homebody. She preferred staying home and hanging out rather than dressing up and going out.

Her best friend Becca was the opposite. If Maddie was a social turtle, Becca was the most colorful butterfly imaginable. Despite being so different, Maddie and Becca usually got along pretty well.

In other words, Becca told Maddie what to do, and Maddie hated confrontation, so she just went along with it. Maddie had been to countless parties with Becca over the years, and she always cowered in a corner until it was over.

Tonight was the same old story: Becca was dragging Maddie to a big costume party in the city. They'd planned on meeting there at the end of the work day, but Maddie was contemplating not going at all. The dense crowds. The flashing lights. The social anxiety. She got a pit in her stomach just thinking about it all.

Her phone buzzed, snapping Maddie out of her thoughts. Speak of the devil, it was a text from Becca: "*You better show up tonight!*"

Maddie sighed. Tapped her fingernail on the counter a few more times. Considered telling Becca she wasn't going.

She could make up an excuse. That might work. She wrote back, *"Work has been crazy today. I've got a pretty bad headache, might not come."*

Becca replied immediately: *"You've used the headache lie before. I know you're trying to worm your way out of this party. I'm not accepting any excuses!"*

Maddie blushed. She'd been found out—her excuses were becoming too predictable. She wrote, *"But I don't even have a costume."*

"You work in a Halloween store!" buzzed a reply. *"Just grab something and meet me there."*

Maddie set down her phone and rubbed her forehead. It looked like there was no way out of this party.

She scanned the sparse shelves. There were barely any costumes left...and they were all the rejects. A few hats, some cheap feather boas, one or two animal masks, and that was pretty much it. So not only was she going to a party she didn't want to attend, but she'd be wearing a lame leftover costume. She groaned. "Terrific."

Time ticked by both slowly and way too quickly for her liking. Soon enough, she couldn't avoid the issue anymore. Her shift at the store was over, which meant she had to head for the costume party.

On her way out the door, she grabbed a random animal mask. She didn't even look to see what it was—if she ignored all things Halloween, maybe it would go away.

But no. As she drove to the party, Halloween was everywhere she looked. Pumpkins, candy, lights, and, of course, costumes. The pit in her stomach solidified even more.

Maddie arrived at the party and parked her car. She supposed she couldn't ignore her costume any longer. She picked up the mask...

And rolled her eyes in frustration.

It was a donkey mask! Of all the animals she could've picked, fate had given her the lamest and ugliest option. Why couldn't she have grabbed something cute, like a cat or a bird?

But it was too late now. People were streaming from the parking lot into the party. Things were already underway. Maddie steeled herself—it was best to dive in and get it over with. She donned the donkey mask and went inside.

The place was loud and crowded already. The plastic mask distorted all the noise, making everything sound as if she were wrapped in tin foil. Her sense of balance was slightly off, and she had to walk with her hands outstretched. Her knees knocked together, and she stumbled to the ground.

Weird. She got nervous in crowds, sure, but she'd never had so much trouble *walking*.

She shook her head, silently repeating her mantra for the night: *Just get it over with.*

Becca recognized Maddie and waved her over to where she stood by the snack table. The consummate social butterfly, she was dressed as a pop star. It was an easy costume for the lovely Becca.

She pulled her friend in for a quick hug, and also to talk over the throbbing music. "Hey, girlie! Glad you came!" She gestured to Maddie's mask. "What are you, a pony?"

Maddie said, "I know, it's lame." The words scraped from her throat, high and somewhat screechy.

She froze.

She hadn't meant to bray like that.

Like a donkey.

Becca laughed it off. "Committing to the costume! I like that. But neighing like that all night will be killer on your voice. Want some punch?"

"Yeah!"

Maddie could hardly get the word out. She'd done it again. As she'd spoken, she'd also honked like an animal. She couldn't help it. The sound had just leapt from her mouth. It felt painful and bizarre...and *wrong*.

She had to be alone for a second. Not wanting to open her mouth again, she held up a finger, then turned from Becca. Filled with embarrassment—and an inkling of fear—she rushed to the bathroom.

She slammed the door behind her and pushed her weight against it. She didn't want anyone else coming in. Not until she'd ripped this horrible mask off her face.

She curled her fingers under the plastic donkey's face and pulled. And pulled. And pulled. But it wouldn't budge. It was stuck to her skin.

The fluorescent lights of the bathroom were making her nauseous. The world spun around her. To keep from falling, she had to get on her hands and knees.

She opened her mouth to call for help...but all that came out was a pathetic bray.

She had to get out of there. Now.

But when she went to open the door and run away, she couldn't.

Her hands had morphed into hooves.

11

Thirst on the 31st

Freaky Factor: 2/3

POPCORN? CHECK.

Cheese puffs? Check.

Two-liter soda all for herself? Big check.

Lara carried the junk food into her living room. There was so much snacking goodness in her arms, she had to use her knees to keep it all steady. Perfect.

She settled onto the couch, splaying all her snacks around. One click of the remote illuminated her giant HD TV. The white glow blinded her for a second.

The rest of the house was dark and quiet. Empty. She smiled as she sank deeper into her couch cushions.

While the rest of the world was bustling around, trick-or-treating and attending festive parties, Lara was spending Halloween exactly how she wanted: watching her favorite horror movie, with piles of junk food at her beck and call.

Lara had a yearly tradition of watching the same movie on Halloween, starting it at midnight. The movie: *Thirst on the 31st*. It was your typical 1980s slasher knock-off, filled with cheap scares and cheaper special effects. Critics and even most audiences said it had no brains or heart whatsoever, but Lara disagreed—victims had their brains and hearts ripped out every few minutes. What the movie lacked in class, it more than made up for in splatter and gore...and Lara loved every goopy minute of it.

She pulled up the movie on the massive TV. As she hit "play," she smiled from ear to ear, ready for some horror-movie chaos.

Lara had a massive soft spot for the movie, having first seen it as a kid. Sure, she knew the plot was paper-thin, the effects were lame, and the sets were made of plywood. What she really loved about *Thirst on the 31st* was its villain.

The Countess Carnage. Iconic. Ruthless. Devious. No one had more fun terrorizing a bunch of teenagers in a creepy old house, or looked better doing it. The Countess would slash an innocent bystander from tip to toe, bathe in their blood, and giggle all the while. She was deliciously evil, bursting with malicious glee, and she made no apology for it. She could fly, sprout claws from her fingertips, and unleash the most bone-chilling laugh in film history.

And, best of all, she won at the end! She successfully tore all those dumb teens to shreds. What's not to love?

The movie's opening credits began to roll, and the musical score filled Lara's dark house. She tossed a cheese puff into her mouth. Let the carnage begin!

Upon this hundredth rewatch, *Thirst on the 31st* was as cheap and bloody as ever. That was part of why Lara loved it so much: It never changed. Same with the Countess. She was consistently diabolical.

Lara smiled thoughtfully as she watched. In her daily existence, she was just a regular person, with a regular job, going about regular life. But she often wondered what it would be like to be the Countess, flying around, terrorizing people, raising bloody chaos with no consequences.

It sounded fun, in a weird way.

Really fun.

As Lara watched, the edges of the screen started to blur. Despite the popcorn and soda, her eyelids grew heavy. Bit by bit, she drifted off to sleep...

...and then jolted awake.

She whipped her head around, wondering what she'd missed. But she wasn't on her couch anymore. The walls were different, replaced with rotting wood. The floorboards creaked beneath her boots. The air was dense with dread.

She was in a creepy old house. She'd never been here before, and yet, it all felt oddly familiar. She knew every detail of this place, from the color of the wood to the sounds of the squeaking rats.

As she glanced left and right, up and down, she caught sight of her hands.

Her fingers had claws.

Lara gasped—she was in *Thirst on the 31st*. Somehow, she'd become a part of her favorite horror movie.

And not only that: She was the Countess Carnage!

Lara began to hyperventilate. She had no idea *what* was happening, *how* it had happened, or *where* she was supposed to go. She just wanted to get home, back to her familiar couch and comforting junk food.

But then she began to float. The Countess could fly, which meant *she* could fly. And then, from elsewhere in the house, she heard a scream. The place was full of hapless teenagers just ripe for the terrorizing.

Slowly, she smiled from ear to ear. She finally had the opportunity she'd been daydreaming about for years. She could live out her fantasy of being a horror movie villain, slashing and scaring with no consequences.

She flexed her claws and released a blood-curdling cackle. This was going to be fun! Off she soared, leaving a trail of dread in her wake.

The next two hours passed in a gleeful fog. Lara zoomed through her favorite movie, scene by gory scene. Not only was she participating in a plot she knew so well, but she was the one driving it! She popped around corners to frighten innocent people. She scraped her claws along the walls, sending splinters into the air.

And she slashed. She tore. She ripped. She spilled buckets of blood, until the decrepit old house had a fresh coat of red paint.

Once the last naive teen was skewered, Lara knew the movie was over. This was how the story ended: The Countess destroyed all the foolish humans and reigned supreme. It was an ending Lara had loved for years—so gutsy for a horror movie to end like that.

And so, Lara the Countess Carnage surveyed her namesake: all the glorious destruction she'd wrought.

The world faded to black. The movie was over. Roll credits.

Lara expected to wake up back home on her couch. But instead, when she next opened her eyes, she was in the old house again.

She didn't have claws for hands anymore. As she assessed herself, she realized she was dressed as one of the victims from the movie.

Cold sweat raced down her forehead. From elsewhere in the house, she heard a bone-chilling laugh. The Countess had begun her hunt.

Before, she'd been the terrorizer. Now, she was the terrorized. And she bet it wasn't going to be nearly as fun this time.

12

Hunger

Freaky Factor: 3/3

"OH MAN!" SAID AMIR as he and his friends wandered their neighborhood. "I hit the motherlode this year."

The chaos of Halloween Night was drawing to a close. Most kids and their parents had completed their trick-or-treating and were already home. Parties were over. Lit porches were darkening. The moon was so high in the black sky, it may have already been November 1st.

But Amir and his buddies still felt that Halloween buzz. They had too much energy to call it a night just yet. They still roamed the streets, headed nowhere in particular.

Amir peered inside his trick-or-treat basket and began to prattle off its sugary inventory: "Let's see... I got chocolate bars and bubble gum and caramels and suckers and popcorn balls—"

One of the other boys rolled his eyes. "We get it, Amir. You got a lot of candy this year."

"I'm not done yet." Amir held up a finger, like a professor giving a lecture, then went on: "And gummies and candy corn and jellybeans and taffy and peanut butter cups..." He shook his basket, searching for any candy he may have missed. "Okay, that's it." His laugh bounced along the asphalt like a stone across water.

His friend sighed again. "What a loudmouth. If you keep bragging about all the candy you got, someone's gonna try to steal it!"

Amir put a hand to his forehead and jokingly lamented, "I can't help it! I just have so much good stuff."

"Smells good..."

Amir didn't recognize that voice. It had trickled from behind them, silky and yet somehow menacing. Like poison.

The group of friends froze in their tracks. Amir's skin prickled with the beginnings of fear, a sense that he was in horrible danger. Slowly, trying to make as little noise as possible, they all turned around.

Standing in the middle of the road was a tall, broad-shouldered man. His face was hidden behind a wolf mask.

Amir tried to remember if he knew this guy's posture or way of speaking...but he came up blank. This was a stranger. Following them. In the middle of the night. Not good.

The masked man tilted his head, studying the boys before him. The air was deathly quiet. No breeze. No birds. There was nothing, as if they were on another planet.

Finally, he spoke again, his tone both smooth and sharp. "I wouldn't mind snacking on a few of those."

Amir shuddered in his shoes, quietly cursing his overflowing basket. He flicked his eyes left and right, hoping to see movement in the windows of the neighboring houses. But it was the dead of night, and everyone was probably asleep. If he called for help, it would take too long for any adults to show up. This masked man could attack them and steal their candy in a matter of seconds.

There was only one option Amir could see.

He steadied himself...inhaled...and screamed, "Run!"

The boys turned from the masked man and bolted down the street. Darkened houses flew by, along with fences, decorations, discarded toys, piles of leaves... The neighborhood looked so normal. It felt bizarre to be running away from someone in such a safe place.

Amir shook his head to clear his thoughts. He had to focus. If his feet got tangled up and he fell, it would all be over.

He didn't hear the man's footsteps, so he risked a peek over his shoulder.

But he was right behind them, running with more grace than Amir knew was possible. His strides were long and loping, like those of an apex predator.

He'd catch up to them within a few breaths. Time to change tactics.

Amir called to his friends, "Everyone split up!"

Part of him hoped at least one of them would stick by his side, but for the first time in their lives, they all listened to him.

Everyone scattered in different directions—down a side-street, through someone's backyard, into a copse of trees. The masked man couldn't catch them all.

This was a good plan. It would work.

Or so Amir silently chanted to himself over and over.

He hopped over a fence and cut across a field. An empty playground lay before him, its seesaw and swings creaking in the eerie moonlight. He ran between the park equipment, making sure not to touch anything—a jangling swing chain would be as good as a neon sign pointing right at him.

He couldn't hear the man's footfalls...but then again, he hadn't before either, and the guy had been mere steps behind them.

He couldn't look back. He had to keep going and hope he'd lost him long ago.

As he exited the neighborhood, he left the streetlamps and porch lights behind him. The darkness made everything so much worse, but he didn't slow down.

With each stride, his trick-or-treat basket jostled in the crook of his arm. He groaned. This stupid candy had caused this whole mess.

Or had it been his loud mouth?

No! It was the psycho in a wolf mask. *He'd* chosen to freak out a bunch of boys. He and he alone was to blame for this.

But regardless of who was to blame, it didn't change the situation. Amir still had to run. So he clenched his jaw and sped up.

He zigzagged through town, past shops and offices long since closed for the night. He turned down alleyways, ducked around fences, sprinted across side-streets...

...and came to a dead end.

A brick wall loomed in front of him, with buildings to his left and right as well. There was nowhere else for him to run. Amir screeched to a stop, panting and shaking.

Hopefully he'd lost the guy.

"I hunger."

Amir turned. The man in the wolf mask stood at the mouth of the alley, a monstrous outline in the waxy moonlight. He had Amir cornered, and he knew it. He strolled forward, slowly, confidently.

"Fine!" Amir had had enough. He threw his basket of candy at the man. "Take it! Take it all!"

But in his gut, he knew that wouldn't fix anything.

The man walked right over the spilled basket of sweets. "That is not what I hunger for."

As the masked man got closer and closer in the claustrophobic alleyway, Amir could feel his hot breath. He could smell his woody musk. And he realized it wasn't a mask at all.

The last thing Amir saw was a flash of teeth.

13

Three Tomorrows

Freaky Factor: 2/3

THERE ONCE WAS A QUIET, studious girl named Annie, who lived a quiet, studious life. From sunup to sundown, from kindergarten to senior year, she focused on her schoolwork. She studied. She looked up new subjects to learn about. She enjoyed reading.

Even her hobbies and freetime were quiet and studious: book clubs, extracurricular projects, and the like. She spoke little and rarely interacted with others. She didn't dislike people—she simply preferred books.

When Annie graduated high school and went off to college, not much changed. She read books. She studied. She focused on attaining her degree and moving on...likely to a quiet, studious career.

Soon enough, her professor announced their first big exam, but Annie wasn't stressed. She was an excellent test-taker and could recall information quite well. But she enjoyed studying, so she took the exam very seriously. Classmates asked her if she wanted to join their study group, but Annie knew she would do better by herself.

The night before her exam, Annie went to the library for one last solo study session. When she entered the library, she found it to be a quiet, studious place. Perfect.

As she roamed the aisles, searching for books that would help her study, her eyes drifted up and down the shelves. Her gaze landed upon a bright red book. There was nothing special about the spine or binding, but the title caught her attention: *Three Truths About Three Tomorrows*.

Annie had never heard of this book, which was odd, because Annie had read most books about many subjects. She pulled the thick volume from its shelf and flicked open the cover.

The first page was blank. As was the second. Annie fanned through the white pages. They were all blank.

Annie nearly put the book back on its shelf, thinking it was a defective copy, but she spied a smudge of ink. The last page of the book held one sentence, the only sentence in the entire volume:

"You will pass your test."

On a whim, Annie checked the book out from the librarian and took it back to her dorm room.

The next day, the test answers came to Annie as if from thin air. After the exam, her fellow students streamed from the classroom, chatting to one another, speculating on how they'd done. But Annie knew she'd passed with flying colors. She had no need to speculate, so she walked back to her dorm alone.

When she was in her room, she exhaled with satisfaction. She'd always been a good student, but today had been different. She wouldn't be surprised if she'd scored a 100%. A thought crossed her mind: Perhaps the strange red book had given her the confidence she'd needed.

She flipped open *Three Truths About Three Tomorrows*. Skimming past the hundreds of bare pages, she arrived at the very end. She gasped—the single sentence had changed. It now said, "You will lose your voice."

She frowned—that didn't inspire much confidence. The book didn't sound so great to her anymore, so she walked to the library to give it back. As she slid it through the return slot, she tried not to watch as the red cover dropped into the dark bin.

The next morning, when Annie got out of bed, she stepped on something hard. It was the red book, lying on the floor, waiting for her.

The hard corner poked into the bare underside of her foot. She opened her mouth to yelp, but no sound escaped her throat.

Fingers trembling, she opened the covers and read a new sentence: "You will disappear."

Annie set off across campus, the book clutched to her chest in fear. When she walked past her teachers and fellow students, no one wondered why she wasn't talking or holding onto a book so tightly. After all, she was a quiet, studious girl.

She needed to get rid of this cursed book, by any means necessary.

She set the book on fire, but it didn't burn.

She tossed it in a lake, but it didn't sink.

So Annie made a decision. She ran far away, trying to escape the book's final truth.

The next day, a professor asked a student where Annie was. The student shrugged. No one knew. She was just gone.

No one looked for her. She was quiet and studious, probably off reading somewhere. She'd turn up eventually.

But she never did. Annie had disappeared.

14

Olympia in Whipple

Freaky Factor: 2/3

THE WAREHOUSE WAS LARGE. Empty. Darker than the bowels of Hell.

A door flew open, and she stumbled in, sweat melding her blonde hair to her face. A sliver of light illuminated the open space, and she cleared her eyes to take it in. She needed a place to hide.

She didn't have much time before the clown caught up to her.

Her heart hammered against her chest like a freight train, making her hands quiver. She reached over and flipped the lightswitch, but only one meager bulb obliged, rapidly flickering on and off, on and off. Laughing at her with wicked glee.

Then, footsteps. Behind her. Big, monstrous footsteps.

The clown.

She gasped, slammed the door shut behind her, and ran deeper into the warehouse. It was dark except for the flickering lightbulb, but at least that meant the clown couldn't see her either.

Keeping her erratic breath as low as possible, she moved into the darkness, searching for a safe haven.

This entire town had been a safe haven for its inhabitants for years. Centuries. Nothing bad ever happened in Krum, Vermont. But ever since this bloodthirsty carnival had set up shop a mere thirty-six hours ago, people had disappeared left and right.

Now she knew. Killers, each and every one of them.

"Oh helloooooo..." A falsetto voice oozed behind her. She spun, and there he was, standing in the doorway.

Zobo the Clown, the carnival called him. Dressed in a garish, rainbow-striped jumpsuit. Big red shoes. Frizzy, colorful hair. Plush nose and white makeup with a permanent smile drawn from ear to ear. Eyes that froze her blood in her veins. A knife clutched in his left fist. Razor-sharp teeth, flashing in the spastic light.

Just minutes before, she'd seen him strangle her best friend with a deflated balloon. She'd screamed and ran, and he'd given chase.

"I found youuuuuuu." The sing-songy tone echoed in the warehouse like a choir from her nightmares. He stepped forward, knife raised.

"No!" She turned frantically, but there was nowhere to run, nowhere to hide. She'd trapped herself. Her feet shuffled backward as she kept her eyes on Zobo, but she stumbled and fell. The bulb kept flickering, and in an instant of darkness, the demented clown was towering over her.

She let loose one last blood-curling scream and held out her hands, though she knew they wouldn't slow the plunge of the knife.

The clown's etched smile widened a bit. "Party's over, princess." And he snuffed her out for good.

"Aaaaaaaand... Scene!"

Huge fluorescent lights—hidden in the darkness amid the overhead rafters—exploded on, flooding every inch of the room with artificial brightness. The dead woman looked like a wax dummy in the overexposure, but nope. Real flesh, real blood, real dead.

Zobo the Clown reached into his mouth and popped out the razor-sharp dentures. They were always agony on his gums. After sighing with relief, he did a quick spot check of his costume. Blood dripped from the knife and his white glove clutching the weapon, and it had splattered halfway up the sleeve. But at least none had gotten on his big floppy shoes—it was torture to scrub blood off those.

"Well done, my friends, well done!" The voice echoed through the room, confident, jovial, the sort of voice that garnered followers. Into the warehouse swept Martin Pinkins, though no one had called him that name in decades. Ever since joining the Olympia Traveling Circus back when disco and Jimmy Carter were popular, he'd been known as Marsuvees the Magnificent, ringmaster extraordinaire.

The crew began to emerge from their hiding spots, chatting amongst themselves:

"Nice work tonight."

"Boy, she was a screamer."

"Didja catch the game last night?"

Zobo ripped off his plush red nose and technicolor wig, and he was Steve once more.

Marsuvees clapped Steve on the back. "How ya feel?"

"Pretty good, pretty good," the boy squeaked. When in costume, Steve could don the persona of a murderous psychopath extremely well, and his shrill voice actually upped the creep factor. In everyday conversation, though, he just came off as a college freshman who'd never gone on a date. Which he was. Major undeclared, working at a killer circus to save up some money for tuition. "Actually, I had a few thoughts..."

"Good!" Marsuvees beamed. He strode into the middle of the room, his cape sweeping behind him like a majestic shadow. He wore black trousers and a waistcoat—both were frayed and rumpled, but they looked lived-in and well-used, not disheveled. A silver pocketwatch dangled from one of the waistcoat's pouches, swinging as he moved. Although his face was lined with wrinkles, his eyes shone like spotlights, and his every step was buoyant. "Alright, crew, circle up!"

The entire cast of the circus slowly entered the room, feet dragging, exhausted after a long day.

Cha-ching-ching ch-ching..

Everyone heard the jingling jewelry before Jasmine the Fortune Mage sauntered in. She stood five feet tall and relished every inch, boasting all the self-assurance of a peacock amongst pigeons. A small silk turban sat atop her head, auburn hair spilling out, and she sported the long, flowing robe of a stereotypical psychic.

Marsuvees spotted Jasmine and waved. "Evening!"

"Hiya, bucko." She winked, her thick Bronx accent clashing with her mystic persona but not caring in the slightest.

The jugglers, ride operators, carnies, and stagehands all gathered around their beloved ringmaster, and he greeted them each by name.

"Debbie, Leah, Rusty, Zeke..." and so on. "Excellent job tonight, everybody!"

Gavin the propmaster was the last to arrive, as per usual. His stomach nearly touched his knees and his bulb wasn't exactly the brightest, but he honestly did his best, and he looked up to Marsuvees like an ant looking up at a mountain.

"Gavin, my main man with the big plan!" Marsuvees pointed finger guns at the portly propmaster.

As the crew yawned and stretched and chatted, Marsuvees reached under his cape and pulled out a checklist on a clipboard. He clicked his pen and muttered to himself, "Let's see..."

Numbers and columns stared back at him. Boxes to be checked off. He stifled a sigh, years of monotony wearing away his zest. So much of his day had been reduced to checking these boxes and crunching numbers.

He shook his head to banish the thoughts, and he put on his smile, his pep, his fire.

"Here in Krum, Vermont, we murdered, lemme see..." He scanned the totals from each horrific attraction. "Thirty-two! Pretty good, crew, pretty good! Jasmine the Fortune Mage killed two in her tent. Good for you, Jazz. The Hall of Mirrors and midway games took out their fair share—gotta love the classics, of course. Our Tilt-a-Whirl took off three heads tonight—the blade is acting up a little bit, so it wasn't as clean a slice as we'd like, but we'll iron that out. We got...three couples in the Tunnel of Love...and one weird lonely guy. That's down from our average, but hey, we've had worse nights, right? And we put that loner out of his misery."

The crew nodded, but it was late. Marsuvees could feel they wanted to get a good night's rest before heading out tomorrow morning.

"Now, notes on the final sequence: Kyle, you picked a good one for the final girl tonight. Young, blonde, attractive. She even tripped a few times and kept looking over her shoulder when Steve was chasing her. It's almost like she was in on it!" He briefly looked over at the body bag. "But of course...she wasn't. That's the beauty of our craft, right, gang? Okay, Steve, nice delivery of the line. Gavin, the lights were flickering way too much."

Gavin looked confused. "They're spooky flickering lights. They're gonna flicker."

"Flicker, yes. But they were like strobes in a nightclub. We want her to be terrified, not have a seizure."

"Aw dangit, one of the breakers must be on the fritz again. I'll check it out." He opened a Sharpie and made a note on his arm.

"Very good, very good. You're a champ, Gavin. Isn't Gavin a champ? Everyone, round of applause for Gavin!" He struck his palms together with vigor, gesturing with his bright eyes for everyone to do the same. Everyone in the circle clapped, but only a few times, with a fraction of Marsuvees's enthusiasm.

"Alright, that's almost everything." He ran down his checklist. "Just a reminder, when we reach our next town, it'll be Jasmine's turn to get the donuts in the morning."

"What town is that?" asked Jasmine.

Marsuvees answered as he lowered his clipboard. "We'll cross into Massachusetts, and we'll set up shop in the small town of Whipple. Be sure to get some Bavarian cream ones. I *love* them in this area."

With that, the crew scattered to their individual closing duties, breaking down the circus only to pack it up and move it to a new town of prey.

Internally, the gregarious ringmaster let out a breath. As much as he loved his colleagues and work, he simply wasn't as young as he used to be. The day had winded him, but he didn't dare let it show. He ran his thumb over the smooth metal surface of the dangling pocketwatch.

"Mr. Magnificent?" Steve meekly approached the ringmaster. "I just... I'd like to talk about the line."

"What, the line? 'Party's over, princess'? You've done great with the line! The delivery sends chills up my spine, I swear."

"Thank you, sir, but... Sir, we've done this same sequence fifty-nine times."

"Exactly! And you've *nailed it* fifty-nine times. In fact, you've gotten better with each performance."

"Well, thank you, sir, but I've been thinking, maybe we can tweak it a little. Like I can have five or six lines I cycle through, and we never know which one I'll say. It'll be kinda exciting, y'know? I've jotted a few down." He dug a small notepad out of his baggy, colorful pants. "How about, 'Knife to meet you'? Or, 'Say cheese...*in hell*'? And then the stab. Also, I've been working on my baritone." He cleared his throat and put on a deep, supposedly menacing voice. "Welcome to your *doooooom—*"

"You're a killer clown, not Macbeth. Stick with the line. Kid, let me tell you, back in my day, I did the exact same sequence eight times a week for *twelve years* straight. You'll settle into it, appreciate the rhythm of it all. Trust me. Now go rest up."

As Steve scuttled away, Marsuvees saw that a long line of performers, crew members, and other assorted carnies were waiting to speak with him. Likely to complain or offer notes about that night's sequence.

He took a breath and sighed, refusing to let his showy smile falter for a moment. A good ringmaster always leant an ear to his performers, for good or for ill.

Marsuvees beckoned forward the next person in line and braced himself for a lot of ill.

• • • •

THE LINE OF PEOPLE wishing to speak with Marsuvees was reaching its end. Good thing, too—he needed a full night's sleep before moving on to the next town in the morning. The key to a solid performance was rest.

Gavin the propmaster was last in line. Marsuvees was glad to see him, since he always had a kind word or two to offer. He needed a little encouragement after being subjected to a whole line of "helpful notes" and "little suggestions." He beckoned Gavin forward.

"Gavin, what can we do about that blade on the Tilt-a-Whirl?" he asked as he walked toward the warehouse's exit.

"Oh, Mars, you know I'd love to fix it. I'd love to patch up the tents, and the rides are rickety as all get-out. And the costumes are older than me and could use an upgrade or two. But there isn't room for any of that in the budget."

Marsuvees exhaled. "That old song..."

"I know, I know, Mars. It bums me out too." Gavin glanced at his shoes for a few steps, but then he perked up. "Shifting tracks, the newsletter came in today."

The ringmaster rolled his eyes. "Oh, is my interview in there *this* time?"

"As a matter of fact..." He smiled and presented Marsuvees with the latest edition of *Maniacs Monthly.*

"Wait, really?" Marsuvees grinned and snatched the paper. Of course, it wasn't on the front, so he flipped it over and read what he'd told the reporter on the phone over a year ago:

There's a side of the world very few know about. And those who find out have one of two outcomes: They either get in on the action, or they become a tally mark on the scoreboard.

This rivalry goes on all over the world. On every continent, in every nation, killers try to rack up the biggest body count.

Creepy mental institutions, scary houses at the end of the block, orphanages, hotels, tourist traps, cabins in the woods, summer camps, traveling circuses... There's a reason these places have become horror clichés in novels, movies, and pop culture. Us.

We killers are a naturally egotistical bunch, so centuries ago, a genius by the name of Ichben Stout founded this system of scorekeeping. He set up a little barbershop in Vienna and went about his business, cutting throats and keeping tally. Then an asylum in Munich caught wind and started keeping track too. A village in England, a carnival in New York, flophouses all over the globe... Everyone wanted in. It caught on like wildfire. Countless years have passed, and naturally, the competition has gotten infinitely stiffer. But we thrive under pressure.

I am ringmaster of the Olympia Traveling Circus, and I have held that title for twenty-nine years. Before that, I was a killer performer in Olympia for almost two decades. We are a proud band of merry miscreants.

So we operate like this. We move from town to town like a real circus and set up our stuff. The big showy tents, the rides, the attractions. We lure in the locals, pop off all we can, and take note of it all, because there are points for style and presentation.

Like, uh... Say we get sixty bodies in one night. That's sixty points off the bat. But the final girl alone could get us a whopping ten points because of all the work we put into her kill—we have flickering lights, obstacles, no cell phone service, and a killer clown who chases her around and says something snappy before he axes her.

I've been doing this a long time, and I know what works and what doesn't. Some of my crew might get complacent or tired or—I hate this *word—bored, but I know what has to be done. We finish with one town, we send in our scores, pack up, and do the same show with the next town.*

We're in the Group Division, which is the most crowded. Scary houses tend to do well on the board. The McManus house in Denton, Texas, in number five overall, which is crazy impressive. The Paris catacombs are number one, because of course they are.

There's also a Singles Bracket, commonly referred to as the Slashers. That's your Leatherfaces, your Buffalo Bills, all those weirdos. I don't care for the Slashers. Why do this sort of work alone?

Traveling circuses are going out of style, but we stick with it. We have our craft, and we respect it. What's our ranking on the board? I don't care—I'm in this for the camaraderie, for the admiration I have for the art.

We are a part of a centuries-long tradition of freaks and killers. We are the Olympia Traveling Circus.

"How is it, Mars?" Gavin was still beside him, breathing far too heavily for standing still.

No matter how hard Marsuvees tried, his hand trembled. His wrinkled, worn, tired hand. The newsletter rattled like a dead leaf. He quickly put on a smile. "Excellent, Gavin. Just excellent." He spun on his heel and walked away, suddenly drained, needing to be alone.

A year. It'd been more than a year since he'd said these things to the newsletter, and nothing had changed. He rifled through his mind, desperately trying to prove himself wrong. But no, it was all the same—the lines, the attitudes, the killings, all of it.

He crumpled the newsletter into a ball and stepped outside the warehouse. The Vermont air was crisp and stung the inside of his nose. He took an even deeper breath, feeling the burn way down in his lungs.

Small towns are all alike, from Texas to Vermont—just swap out salsa for chowder. Restless citizens willing to let in any traveling attraction that promises to stir up a shred of excitement. Citizens who mourn those missing whenever the attractions leave but give up looking for them after two to three weeks. Such short attention spans are the bread and butter of this gig.

Marsuvees pushed back his hair, feeling a few strands come loose between his fingers. He was getting old. Past his prime. Restless, just like the people in the thousands of towns he'd terrorized throughout his career.

He didn't want to admit it, but he couldn't remember if he'd been to Krum before. He assumed not, since they weren't chased out of town with torches and shotguns, but it sure looked familiar. A Main Street with lame antique stores and barbers and such. An out-of-date McDonald's. A public school with a few fields for sports... These details could describe every single town he'd visited in the last fifty years.

A pinch of shame poked at him. He should be grateful to have this job. Especially in this economy. And he loved the people he worked with—Jasmine, Gavin, Steve, everyone. His cape still fit well, even if it was a bit frayed and musty. His voice was loud and likable day after day, and age had barely affected his bones and joints.

But a change of pace would be nice.

"Hey, Mars." Jasmine the Fortune Mage joined him outside. She held a pack of cigarettes, but it was still in the shrink-wrap. Her concerned eyes told the whole story: She'd seen him crumple up the newsletter. For a world-class performer, her face sure revealed her real emotions. "Howyadoin?"

He smirked in spite of his melancholy. Her Bronx accent clashed with the fortuneteller get-up like a menorah in a mosque. "Jazz, how long have you been doing this?"

She fiddled with the plastic on the pack as she thought. "Hmm... I got my first gig with the Harvest Festival in Buhl, Idaho. My kill numbers were high enough that I got poached by a traveling group called Cirque Mystique. I met my first husband there, so it's been...thirty-some years." She popped out a cigarette. "You?"

Marsuvees held the pocketwatch in his hand and looked out at Krum. "A good deal longer than that."

"Yeah, I can see the salt in your hair. This tires ya, I know. The tours, the dates, the schedules. But hey, no one on this earth or any other is a better ringmaster than you. The crew loves ya."

"Back in the day"—Marsuvees clutched the sides of his cape with both hands—"I lined the edge of this cape with garrote. If I swung it just right, with a careful flick of the wrist..." He spun with a grand flourish, the cape whipping around him with a crack. "I could take an arm clean off, maybe a head if the angle was dead-on."

"Oh, hun, back in my prime, you shoulda see my bag of tricks." She beamed at the memories. "I'm pretty rusty nowadays, but back then, I was a real pro at what my costume suggests. Entrancement, light hypnotism, suggestion. Boy oh boy, the things I could make 'em do." She sagged. "Now I just smash crystal balls on suckers' heads."

The ringmaster grinned. "Remember Asheville? One of the big rigs broke down, so we only had half of our props and sets. And on top of that, a bunch of our performers had the flu!"

"Yeah, yeah, but the show must go on, right?"

"Exactly. We were operating at low levels, and some of those townsfolk almost got the best of us."

"They were scrappy, that's for sure." Jasmine took off her turban and auburn wig, letting her stringy gray hair tickle down her neck. "We were close to being history with that one."

"But we rallied. Came together and showed them who's the best killer carnival in the world."

A pause. The night breathed, stars shimmered.

Crickets chirped, then fell silent.

"That was, what..." Jasmine chewed on her cigarette. "...a decade ago?"

Marsuvees deflated. His shoulders slumped, and he felt every year of his life. "Yes, something like that." He straightened his waistcoat.

"Get some rest, Jazz. You did well today. Be ready to move on in the morning."

Jasmine nodded and turned to leave. But she hesitated and looked at the dashing, dispirited man once more. "Martin Pinkins, I've never encountered a man so beloved by his acquaintances."

The ringmaster clutched the pocketwatch, eyes downcast. "Marsuvees." He shot Jasmine a glance. A very brief glance. "Please."

The walls of the creepy warehouse tilted to their sides, and members of the Olympia crew carried them away to the trucks. Tomorrow, they'd be set up again in Olympia, just as they had been in hundreds upon hundreds of other towns.

· · · ·

THE CARAVAN OF TRUCKS, trailers, and sedans rumbled to a stop on the side of an empty road. Marsuvees was leading the Traveling Circus in his amber-colored Ford Escort, and he'd needed to change his oil since they'd passed through Virginia months back. He put the car in park, the gearshift groaning at him, and rubbed his eyes.

It'd been a long night of driving—just like every night for the past several decades. Back roads through forests and fields provided little entertainment for the dazed driver, but Marsuvees was an old pro at staying awake behind the wheel. It used to be upbeat music: Earth Wind & Fire, that sort of thing. As he'd gotten older, he'd found that Red Bull and Spree really gave him a good buzz for endless nights on the road.

He opened the door and unfolded himself from the Escort's grip. The sun was just peeking over the trees, the sky varying shades of pale yellow, pale blue, and pale white. It was going to be a beautiful Massachusetts morning, especially out here in the middle of nowhere. There was hardly a sound, except for the breeze tickling the forest, the occasional birdcall, the scurrying of little paws.

He gazed at the halted convoy behind him as all the drivers and passengers also got out to stretch. Carnies falling out of cars, yawning, scratching, smelly, and unshaven—it was the essence of a traveling circus, and Marsuvees loved every ounce of it.

The ringmaster mentally shoved his fatigue into a box and beamed at the line of carnies, sweeping his arm. "Olympia, welcome to Whipple!"

A quaint wooden sign repeated his greeting. The "*Welcome*" was written in cursive, the "*Whipple*" in bold, bright letters. Bushy foliage and a blue river decorated the background, but the etching made it all pop. Despite being located on the side of a small, uninhabited road, the paint was vibrant and electric, as if it'd been applied just yesterday.

Marsuvees continued to address his crew. "Population: three hundred. A drop of civilization surrounded by forestry. We're still about a mile out from the town proper." He smiled and dramatically cupped his ear. "No neighboring towns. No casual passersby. No one but the deer and the hawks to hear the people's screams." He clapped once, and the sound echoed through the air for several moments. "Oh what fun!"

The crew muttered amongst itself. Marsuvees squinted at the sun peering over the trees. Morning was well underway. Time to explore their new hunting grounds.

He pressed a hand down his waistcoat and trousers, which were hopelessly rumpled after hours in the driver's seat. His eyes found Gavin's in the crowd.

The propmaster jogged to the front of the caravan. Gavin had been driving one of the big rigs, with Steve in the cab as his passenger. Gavin stopped dutifully before Marsuvees, huffing and puffing but attentive. Steve also picked his way through the crowd on pins and needles, his legs awkwardly stiff.

"Gavin," Marsuvees said, peaking his eyebrows, "care to join me?" He asked this exact question at every town before the set-up.

Gavin replied as always, "Right behind ya!" His pants sagged under the weight of his tool belt, but he was ready to go.

"Hold on!" squeaked Steve. He waddled up to Marsuvees, his face contorted as if passing a kidney stone.

"Oh, right..." Gavin lowered his voice. "The kid has needed the john for the past fifty miles."

Jasmine sauntered by, her jewelry as jingly as ever. "Cantcha just unzip behind a tree, kid?"

Steve held the sides of his gut as if he might actually split in two. "It's solid, not liquid."

"Squat, then," she said.

The college kid looked aghast. And slightly embarrassed. "I'm not an animal."

Gavin muttered, "You've smelled like one for the past fifty miles."

"Okay, okay." Marsuvees waved his hands, regaining control of the conversation. "We'll walk into town. I'll meet some of the higher-ups, schmooze and groove and dazzle them all, get them excited to come out to the Olympia tomorrow. Gavin, you snoop around a bit, measure out where we'll put the tents, rides, and spooky warehouse. You know the drill. Steve, find a toilet."

"I know that drill," he nodded.

"Alright, gents," Jasmine straightened her turban and auburn locks, "let's get struttin'."

Steve's eyes widened. "You're coming too?" He clenched his legs harder.

"I've been in that frickin' PT Cruiser for as long as I can remember. You're not leaving without me."

Marsuvees smirked and grabbed his cape from the backseat. He fastened it around his neck and let it unfurl majestically. "I'm ringmaster of this circus! I cannot allow this town's first impression of me to be inferior to that of anyone else. Not even Jasmine the Fortune Mage."

Jasmine chuckled and looped her arm around the caped man's. "Lead the way, Mars."

• • • •

WHIPPLE, MASSACHUSETTS. The place was as picturesque as a Norman Rockwell snapshot. Houses and buildings teleported directly from the '50s lined the streets. Shrubs and lawns were manicured with precise care. American flags hung from almost every structure. Silver trashcans sat on curbsides, bikes leaned against mailboxes, and Marsuvees didn't see a single piece of stray litter.

The four carnies walked along Main Street, a river of asphalt that bisected the town and held its greatest attractions. The marble steps of City Hall, the redbrick public library, a barber shop, and several diners and antique stores lined either side. At the end of the road towered what was clearly the central hub: a whitewashed church with a tall steeple and brass bell.

The ringmaster took a deep breath through the nose and caught whiffs of apple pie, barbeque sauce, and cozy fires pluming from chimneys.

"Ain't this quaint?" Jasmine exhaled some smoke of her own. She flicked her stubby cigarette into a nearby shrub.

"Nothing looks open," Steve lamented, still hobbling in agony.

Marsuvees continued to study Main Street. The redbuds were in full bloom, the asphalt black as midnight. Each painted surface was flawlessly smooth, without a single bubble or defect. It was as if this town had been grown and perfected in a petri dish. Every little detail was positioned just so. Yet, not a single living soul was in sight.

A cold breeze made him shiver, and he drew his cape closer. "Gavin, start scouting for good places to set up. Close to the edge of town, near the road."

"You got it, boss." Gavin wiped a brow, hitched up his pants, and turned down a small side-street. He pulled a huge measuring tape from his tool belt and ambled away from the group.

"*Mama Rose's Fresh Apple Pies...*" Jasmine read a sign hanging in a small shop window. "*Just remember, keep your eyes on the pies.*" She groaned.

Steve cackled. "Now that's good."

Jasmine massaged her temples.

"It's... You see, it's like *prize—*"

"I get it, numbnuts, it's just stupid."

"Well, hello there!" The vocal embodiment of sunshine echoed from behind them.

Marsuvees, Jasmine, and Steve whipped around. Standing in the middle of the street, about twenty yards away, was a tall woman in a navy skirt and blazer. Her curly hair bounced, and Marsuvees worried her wrist would snap from her jubilant waving.

She wore high heels, but he hadn't heard any footsteps. He shook his head to clear the random thought and donned his ringmaster charm. "Hello to you too, madam! My name is—"

The woman cut off his pitch: "Welcome to Whipple, the smallest town with the biggest heart! We're so glad you decided to stop in today. I'm Rhonda, and it's my sincere pleasure to serve as the mayor of this little patch of heaven!"

The ringmaster jumped in as soon as she finished talking: "It's *our* pleasure to make your acquaintance, Rhonda! I am Marsuvees the Magnificent!" He cracked his cape, which echoed up and down the empty street. "I am the ringmaster and harbinger of the one and only Olympia Traveling Circus! From coast to coast, none other can provide the thrills we can!"

"Well, we're certainly happy you're here." Rhonda's pearly smile grew even bigger. "Whipple is such a one-of-a-kind town. Our citizens truly are the salt of the earth, and you won't find better home-cooking anywhere else! Up here, we love each other, our country, and our pie. In that order!" She giggled. "Be sure to stop by the Whipple History Museum, housed in our old schoolhouse built in 1795!"

Marsuvees's nose twitched. He'd been a showman for decades, and he knew when he was being sold something. He cleared his throat. "My colleagues and I are certainly taken with your town." He strolled toward the mayor, and Jasmine and Steve followed. "It would be my greatest honor to invite you and all your residents to partake in our flight of fancy tonight, once we set up our wares. Olympia is an experience second to none!" He stopped a few feet in front of the woman. All his life, he'd been accustomed to towering over most people, but Rhonda's eyes looked directly into his.

Her warm, brown eyes.

Had she blinked yet? Marsuvees couldn't remember. She had to have.

"Aren't you just a peach?" She squeezed the ringmaster's cheek, and he nearly recoiled out of instinct, but his showman charm forced him to beam at her. "Let me show you around a bit." She swept her arm toward Main Street, and Marsuvees turned to see what she was gesturing to.

All at once, every door to every shop swung open and a person stepped out. Bakers, florists, barbers, teachers, old ladies, little boys, moms and dads—they all smiled at the three visitors from the traveling circus and called out a greeting.

"Hiya, strangers!"

"Pleased to meetcha!"

"Welcome!"

"Hello over there!"

As if a switch had been flipped, the town came to life. People bustled down the sidewalk—couples walking golden retrievers, a group of girls playing hopscotch, a milkman carrying a crate on his shoulder.

Kids on bikes rolled between buildings, and a pastor in a cardigan peeked out from the church's window and waved.

The three carnies stared. It was like a Disneyland attraction: very lifelike and tactile, but still plainly artificial.

Jasmine leaned toward Marsuvees and whispered, "When was the last time you saw a kid playing hopscotch?"

Steve added, "Or an actual milkman?"

The townsfolk moved back and forth across Main Street with stilted, choreographed steps. Marsuvees narrowed his eyes and looked closer. The clothing was freshly pressed, the paint bright and new, the flowers blooming in cold winter.

He turned to Rhonda. "So what's your ranking?"

The mayor's megawatt smile didn't falter for a moment, but she paused, like a computer rebooting. "Then we're dropping the pretense, Mr. Marsuvees?" Her voice was still syrupy, but layered with a dark confidence.

Steve's jaw dropped wide open and dangled in the breeze.

"If you'd like," Marsuvees continued. "I've been doing this since you were in diapers, so you're not likely to lull me into any sort of security."

Rhonda shrugged in a folksy, 'aw-shucks' manner and laughed. "In that case, will you and your cohorts do me the great honor of joining me for a little breakfast? Roy's Diner makes the fluffiest pancakes in the world."

Jasmine began to speak, but Marsuvees got there first. "We'd love to. Breakfast sounds wonderful, but we must get back to our crew soon after."

The mayor clapped in elation. "Excellent! Please follow me."

The foursome walked down Main Street. Rhonda's long strides forced Jasmine to pick up the pace, which the fortuneteller clearly resented.

Rhonda raised her voice to the citizens on Main Street. "Whipple, this was an excellent rehearsal! I'd like you all to meet a few members of the Olympia Traveling Circus! They're in the same business we are, and they will be visiting for a brief time."

Marsuvees expected the Whipplians to deflate, grumble, and sulk back into their shops, but the exact opposite happened. Their smiles and greetings brightened all the more. They swarmed around the three carnies, walking alongside them like cheery tour guides.

"Glad you're here, Olympia!"

"It's so neat to make your acquaintance!"

"Can you give us some tips on showmanship?"

"How do *you* get blood out of polyester?"

These people truly loved their job, and they were happy to welcome the strangers. The ringmaster hadn't seen that sort of positive attitude from Olympia since...

He couldn't remember.

"Mars," Jasmine hissed. Her muscles were tight as she walked next to him, eyes darting from smile to smile. "What are we *doing*? These people are nutbags, and they're *murderous* nutbags."

"Like us," Marsuvees said.

"Exactly!" She looked around and brought her volume back down. "We need to get back in our trucks and drive far, far away from this freaky-deaky Mayberry."

Steve nodded. "I'm with her. Freaky-deaky Mayberry."

Marsuvees held out his hands to staunch their protests. "Jazz, Steve, we're professionals. We'll pay our respects, charm them a bit, build our reputation, and be on our merry way."

The fortune mage and the college kid exchanged worried glances, but Marsuvees sauntered tall, his cape billowing in his wake. He knew it was hard to doubt a man in a cape, and sure enough, the two followed close.

A shadow of guilt prodded his heart, because they both made a solid point. But the people of Whipple seemed so content. Their happy-go-lucky persona wasn't a mere façade—it was a mindset, a genuine demeanor. For all his pomp and flash, "Marsuvees the Magnificent" was just a character. A mask.

He wanted to be around honest satisfaction, if only for a single breakfast.

So Marsuvees the Magnificent straightened his waistcoat and donned a winning smile, ignoring the doubts of his colleagues.

Rhonda turned her smile to Jasmine as they walked. "I love your outfit," she said to the fortune mage. "All the sequins and jingle bells. It's so cute!"

Jasmine ruffled. "It's not supposed to be cute..."

"Here we are!" Rhonda led them to the entrance of a diner ripped straight out of the Eisenhower era without a hint of pastiche. "It'll be my treat, okie dokie? I just love sharing what I love with the people I love." She swung open the door, which chimed, and strutted right in like she owned the place.

Marsuvees, Jasmine, and Steve followed closely behind. The smells from the kitchen were heavenly, and Mars realized that his nightly feast of Red Bull and Spree didn't hold a candle to a real breakfast, cooked by real people, in a real town.

He was starting to like it in Whipple.

Rhonda's heels clacked across the linoleum floor to a booth in the back corner. She smirked over her shoulder to her guests. "This is my usual table. Slide on in!"

They all sat down, Rhonda on one side of the table, Marsuvees, Jasmine, and Steve facing her. Dozens of Whipple citizens poured into the diner and filled every possible seat, chattering and laughing and peeking curiously at the circus people every now and then.

A jolly elf of a man pranced by their table. "The usual, mayor?"

A nod of bouncy hair. "You got it, Roy!"

Steve fidgeted in his seat, clutching his knees.

"Kid," Jasmine groaned, "there's gotta be a bathroom in this joint."

"I can hold it," he squeaked. "I'm starving."

"So, Mr. Magnificent," the mayor beamed at the ringmaster, "have you ever run into a group of fellow troublemakers like us?"

"Let me think..." Marsuvees smoothed his graying temples as if massaging his memory. "Back in the '80s, I passed by a summer camp in New Jersey that liked to pick off the teenagers. Big crazy guy in a hockey mask with a blade. Not nearly as welcoming as you folks, so we moved right along."

"Yeah," Jasmine added, "I once crossed paths with those creepy Bigfoot impersonators in Oregon. Lemme tell ya, they do *not* like people stepping into their neck of the woods. Most killers see other killers as competition. Y'know, rivals."

"Oh my." Rhonda's eyes widened and she placed a hand to her heart. "How horrific!"

Steve's forehead creased. "But you guys are in our same business, right?" He looked around, a bit lost. "I mean, killing people?"

"Oh yes!" She smiled and nodded pleasantly. "Now, I'll be quite honest with you all, we're new at it. To tell the truth, I'm so gosh-darn nervous talking business with big shots like you."

Marsuvees puffed out his chest. "We all started somewhere. Just stick with it."

The owner of the diner revved back to their table and plopped a plate in front of each of them. Simple buttered toast for the mayor, but a feast for the out-of-towners: scrambled eggs, bacon, and plump blueberry muffins. Even Jasmine looked won over by the spread.

"Dig in!"

No one had to tell Steve twice. He snatched up a fork and began shoveling eggs into his mouth.

Marsuvees ignored the food for the time being. He felt in his element, talking about the business from a place of experience. "Just how long have you been doing this, Rhonda?"

"Two weeks." Her permanent smile glistened in the diner's yellow light.

Jasmine put down her utensils, suddenly interested. "Two *weeks*? Dang, girl, you weren't kidding. You *are* new at this."

"Oh yes, a young couple got lost among the trees on the outskirts of our town. They came to charge their telephones, and I ran them over with my car a couple times. Not very stylish, right?" She giggled. "No, we lack the showmanship you flaunt so wonderfully, Marsuvees. I've been practicing that little speech I greeted you with for days!"

"No worries, madam, you're well on your way!" Marsuvees smiled, and the townsfolk rippled with delight.

"We're very excited to get started." Rhonda picked up her toast. "In fact, after today, I think we'll jump right to the top of the leaderboard in our region."

"Why's that?" asked Jasmine.

"Well, I don't think a group of killers has ever taken out another group before." She took a bite with a *crunch*.

Marsuvees froze. "Pardon?"

"Imagine the headline of the next edition of *Maniacs Monthly*: *Fledgling Whipple topples old Olympia*!"

Blood pumped through Marsuvees's veins like a raging river. He squared his shoulders and leaned forward, eyes blazing. "You will want to choose your next words very carefully, madam."

"Oh, I have! Believe you me, our town will find no pleasure in dispatching your... What was it? Your proud band of merry miscreants." She twittered and swallowed the last bit of toast. "I read your interview in the newsletter just yesterday, and when our scouts saw the Olympia trucks parked outside our little town... I just knew it was a sign! You'll be our bridge to success!"

Marsuvees tensed his muscles, ready to shove the table against the mayor and make a run for it. But his knees felt like they were full of glass, and the cold weather had stiffened his joints. The diner was packed full of Whipple citizens, all of them watching. Waiting. Smiling.

The Olympians stood no chance. For the first time in years—decades, even—Marsuvees the Magnificent felt the icy tendrils of fear.

"Wow." Rhonda stared at the three of them in awe. "It's still hitting me. The Olympia Traveling Circus! I'd never heard of you before yesterday, but judging from your interview, you must be in the top ten! I have nothing but respect for everyone in this business. If it helps your death go down a little easier, you'll be revered in this town for years to come."

Jasmine's rough exterior finally cracked, and she began to tremble. "Mars..." she whimpered. "This isn't where I want to die."

Rhonda sat ramrod straight with the eyes of a tyrant and the smile of a clown. "You said it yourself, Marsuvees the Magnificent: We all start somewhere. And today, you will end here."

Steve looked up for the first time in several minutes, his plate licked clean. "Wait, what's going on?"5

Jasmine gulped. "Freaky-deaky Mayberry is gonna kill us, kid."

A bit of egg dribbled from the college kid's lip.

Marsuvees cleared his throat and tried to flip through all possible scenarios for their demise. If he could get ahead of their plan, he might be able to find an escape route. If he were in their position, how would he dispatch the newcomers?

"Is it the food, Rhonda? Small-town diner, eggs and muffins, made with love and arsenic? That has to be worth a few style points on the board."

The mayor looked truly shocked and aghast. She stammered before speaking. "We in Whipple *love* Roy's Diner. It is a lynchpin of our community. I have been entirely honest with you, Olympia, and I meant it when I said I wanted to share what I love." She reined in her outburst and straightened her blazer. "Now, if you all will come with me outside, we will commemorate your visit to our terrific tiny town."

The three circus performers rose from their seats on shaky legs and followed the grinning gremlin. Happy faces glared at them from all sides, as if they were gladiators in some sort of demented coliseum.

Which, it struck Marsuvees, they pretty much were.

Killing for sport. On any other day, he would swell with pride and give a momentous pep talk to his crew, likening Olympia to Rome's greatest warriors and entertainers.

Today, however, they were the victims. Fodder for the real pros.

Sweat trickled down his back despite the frigid air. They exited the diner and walked up Main Street. So much had changed over the course of the breakfast, which, according to the crumbs on Steve's chin, was admittedly delicious.

"Right this way," Rhonda led them down a side-street behind the redbrick library. Stacks upon stacks of paint cans stood in the alleyway.

"Got enough paint?" Jasmine growled.

"We touch up the town every morning, especially the signs announcing our town limits. We never know when guests will drop in, and we want to be as warm and welcoming as possible."

As much as Marsuvees tried, he couldn't fully contain his professional curiosity. "How'd you get the redbuds to bloom in winter?"

"Super glue. Now, if you please..."

Three things awaited the Olympians and Whipplians behind the library:

A huge, vibrant mural painted on the back of the building, depicting sunshine and lush forestry, along with bold lettering that said, *"Wish You Were Here!"*

A gallows with three nooses ready to go, set up in front of the mural.

And an old-fashioned camera on a stand, presumably to capture the moment.

"Well, crap," Jasmine rustled. She then remembered something and turned to the college kid. "Oh yeah. Sorry, Steve."

"I don't have that problem anymore," Steve whimpered. His eyes were locked on the wooden gallows. Face pale. Knees trembling. Utterly terrified.

Marsuvees glared at Rhonda. "This will rack up a lot of style points, huh? Making a postcard?"

The mayor nodded exuberantly. "You betcha! Now, up up up!"

The crowd closed in around the three Olympians, blocking their every escape route. Slowly, dejectedly, Mars, Jazz, and Steve climbed the wooden stairs of the gallows and each stood on a trapdoor under a noose. The boards were smooth and firm. Freshly constructed, Mars guessed, just like the rest of the town.

Roy the diner-owner walked behind Steve and looped the noose around his scrawny neck. The college kid balled his fists to keep them from shaking. His voice was barely audible when he squeaked, "I just wanted to be a serious actor..."

Marsuvees glanced at Steve. "That's why you kept working on the line? 'Party's over, princess'?"

Steve nodded, his eyes welded shut.

The cold nipped at Marsuvees's muscles as he stared at the crowd of Whipplians. A sea of smiling faces stared back, unblinking and completely placid, as if they were watching an orchestra perform in the park.

Next, Roy tried to fit the noose around Jasmine's neck, but her sequined turban was too cumbersome. It occurred to Marsuvees that this was the first time Roy had ever performed the duty of hangman. This was Whipple's very first killing, and they were still working out the kinks. Eventually, Roy ripped off her turban and flung it behind him, taking her auburn wig with it. Her stringy gray hair fell across her face as the rope tightened against her throat.

A flicker of movement caught Marsuvees's attention. Not from the crowd of Whipplians. But, rather, from behind them. He scanned the streets...

...and saw him.

Gavin, peeking around a corner. His massive girth made it difficult for him to remain incognito, but the entire town's attention was on the gallows. He locked eyes with Mars and held out a hand as if calming a braying horse.

Marsuvees wanted to shout and leap and run, but the rope was already around his neck. Gavin cocked his head and ducked out of sight.

Rhonda's clacking heels snapped Marsuvees's attention away from the hidden Olympian. "Face the camera, everyone! If you can't see it, it can't see you! So, my guests, are you ready?"

"Do we have a choice?" growled Jasmine.

"Nope!" She let loose a giddy sigh. "Honestly, friends, I would like to say one last time that it has been a true honor meeting and murdering you today. We couldn't have done it without you. Okay, Frank, ready the camera. Now, everyone say *cheese*!"

Marsuvees clutched his pocketwatch in his palm.

The trapdoors opened.

The camera popped with a flash of smoke.

The three-hundred townsfolk said "*cheese*" through their grinning teeth.

And Marsuvees, Jasmine, and Steve dropped.

Gravity yanked Marsuvees toward the ground, the firm wooden boards no longer under his feet. For a moment that felt like an eternity, the ringmaster of Olympia plummeted through the air, his cape billowing like a bat's wings. His heart held its breath, waiting for the rope to become taut and snap his neck like a twig.

Then, his feet hit the pavement. Unprepared, his knees buckled, and he collapsed in a heap. He took a deep breath. The cold oxygen tasted sweet.

He looked around, frantic, confused, lost in the whirlwind. He was lying under the gallows, pale sunlight seeping between the floorboards above. The three trapdoors hung open.

The noose dangled from his neck, limp and useless. It hadn't been fastened to the beams above him. He'd simply fallen through a square hole.

He should be dead.

But Gavin, that brilliant propmaster, had been a step ahead.

"Holy crap..." Jasmine's Bronx accent whispered in the shadows. "What in the world...?"

Mars squinted. Jasmine had landed with a thud next to him, buttocks no doubt horribly bruised, but no worse for the wear. Her noose was tangled up in her jangly dress. Steve sat next to her, his open trapdoor shining a spotlight on him. His eyes were still clenched shut, and he was hyperventilating.

The Whipplians were still saying "*cheese*" for the camera outside the gallows. No one had noticed yet that the nooses had come loose.

"Steve," Marsuvees hissed, but the college kid kept breathing like a piston. "*Steve*, we're alive, but we have to move *now*!"

"Wh-What?" Steve inched his eyes open and slapped a hand to his chest to feel his heart beating. "Are you sure?"

"What dumb question is that?" Jasmine tore away her noose and jostled to a crouched position.

"Come on." Marsuvees followed suit. "Gavin gave us a window of opportunity, and we can't waste it."

"Wait wait wait." Steve started to stand, but his legs were still shaky from the adrenaline of an extremely-near-death experience. "Where are we going? There's a hundred psychopaths right outside this stupid wooden death box!"

"The kid makes a point."

Mars wiped sweat and dust from his forehead with the back of his sleeve. "Gavin is behind the building at our two o'clock. We'll just have to make a run for it."

Jasmine and Steve shook their limbs in preparation to sprint. Marsuvees held his hands in a cradle, preparing to boost them through his trapdoor. They all locked gazes for a moment.

Just a moment.

Out in front of the gallows, the townsfolk finished their "*cheese.*" Mars could hear them laughing, chitchatting, and back-slapping each other. It was only a matter of seconds before someone noticed the distinct lack of swinging corpses.

"Go."

Jasmine stepped in his hands and launched herself back into the sunlight, Steve directly behind her. The two reached back into the hole, grabbed Mars's arms, and heaved him along.

Suddenly, less than a minute after dropping through the trapdoors, they were back on the gallows, squinting in the sun, looking out at the citizens of Whipple. The merry would-be-murderers didn't even notice. They were too busy conversing amongst themselves:

"That went really well for our first time!"

"Rhonda's just the tops, isn't she?"

"Care to grab some ice cream after this?"

But a moment later, the Olympians' luck ran out. Frank, the Whipplian man behind the camera, gaped and pointed at the three breathing bodies on the gallows. "Uh, that's not how it's supposed to be..."

They didn't have a second to spare. Marsuvees bounded off the platform into the heart of the crowd. He shoved bodies out of the way, and he could hear Steve and Jasmine doing the same.

No one moved. No one tried to grab them. They looked on, mere bystanders, deer in headlights.

Just as Marsuvees had gambled. No one had physically forced the three of them onto the gallows—the town's horde-like presence had prodded them under the nooses. When push came to shove and someone did something counter to their wishes, their inexperience betrayed them.

"*What are you doing?*" Rhonda bellowed with sunshiny rage. "They're getting away!"

Twenty paces. The Olympians were a mere twenty paces away from being able to turn out of sight.

"You *morons*!"

Ten paces. Cape fluttering. Dress jingling. Feet pounding.

"Get your cars, cover the exits out of town. We'll catch them!"

They skidded around the corner to find Gavin waiting. He joined their sprint.

Marsuvees slapped the propmaster's back. "Gavin, my main man with the big plan! I love you, buddy."

"Always, Mars," Gavin huffed and puffed. "I saw that gallows when I was scoping out where we could put our tents, and I figured something was wonky."

"That's one way to put it!" Jasmine moved her short legs as fast as her dress would allow.

They were back on Main Street, running the opposite direction they'd meandered just a half-hour earlier. The barbershop, the diners, the silver trashcans, and the perfectly manicured lawns... All a mask.

Tires squealed in the distance, and Marsuvees's nerves tingled. From all directions came the sounds of people yelling and car doors slamming, an army assembling for attack.

"We need to get off the street. Take cover."

"Mars," Jasmine pressed, "we need to *get out of here*. The rest of our crew is sitting a mile away. We can make it!"

"There are three hundred of them and four of us. We may have slipped past them once, but Rhonda won't let that happen again. We need to get out of sight and think!"

Jasmine gritted her teeth but followed the ringmaster as he detoured toward one of the antique shops. A plastic sign reading *CLOSED* hung on the glass door, but he shoved it open and waved his three friends inside.

He scanned Main Street before closing the door. The coast was clear...for the time being. He could hear car engines revving as the bloodthirsty townsfolk took position all over Whipple. He exhaled and ducked inside.

The shop was dusty but arranged with OCD-like care. Shelves were full of old vases, toys, and crap no one wanted, along with racks and racks of clothes. An ancient grand piano wilted in the corner, untouched for God-knows-how-many years. The whole store must be a façade, set up with just enough authenticity to convince a passerby.

The four carnies huddled behind the checkout counter, panting and trembling. All was quiet except for their fearful breaths. Dust motes floated through the sunbeams like trapeze artists.

"Mr. Magnificent," Steve squawked. "We're gonna die, aren't we?"

Pause. No one disputed him.

He went on, quietly, more to himself than his fellow Olympians. "Now I know what the final girl feels like when I chase her through the warehouse."

Gavin chuckled softly. "No flickering lights, though."

Steve guffawed, then slapped a hand over his mouth to stifle the noise.

Jasmine rubbed her eyes. "Wish I had one last cig. But I guess now's as good a time as any to quit."

Gavin looked around at his friends, tears welling in the corners of his eyes. "It's been a pleasure serving you performers. I never had the stagey knack, but I'm honored I got to make you all look good."

"We are not dying," Marsuvees said plainly. Confidently. Boldly.

Everyone looked at him with tired eyes. Eyes ready to give up.

"My wife was Olympia's finest contortionist. Gilda the Great." He spread his hands as if presenting a marquee, his gaze staring far away into the past. "The shapes she made boggled my mind. She could strangle a man with each appendage...simultaneously! And our little girl had a knack for training animals. She loved birds the most, and she dreamed of having her own show one day. Doves, eagles, jays, all flying around over the audience, pecking out their eyes." Marsuvees smiled at the thought, but it was just a distant dream.

He squared his shoulders and looked each of his friends in the eye. "I love this circus. My girls loved it too. And there's no way some dopey little town of slap-happy morons is going to get the best of us."

A car cruised down Main Street, smiling Whipplian faces in each window, searching for the runaway carnies. It passed the antique shop.

"Look, we're old. We're past our prime. We've failed. But you know what else? We're experienced. We've been through the muck. We know what works and what doesn't. We've seen the face of failure, spat in it, and kept going anyway. That's why we're still here, and that's why we'll see tomorrow."

Gavin said what he'd never dared say: "Boss, we've been at the bottom of the rankings for years."

Marsuvees opened his silver pocketwatch, and two small faces smiled back at him. An old photo was housed between the watch's jaws, near to him at all times. The two women he would lasso the moon for. Gilda the Great and Rosalind the Greatest.

He snapped the watch shut. "We don't need to win all the time. Just today."

With that, Marsuvees stood up and strode over to the browbeaten grand piano. He threw open the lid, scattering dust and dirt. With an old veteran's eye, he examined the strings—they sagged but were still in good condition. "Just allow me to do a bit of tailoring first."

· · · ·

MARTIAL LAW HAD ENVELOPED Whipple, Massachusetts. A sickly-sweet, perpetually smiling martial law. Sedans and vans blocked all roads leaving town. Residents strolled the sidewalks, walking their dogs, eating caramel apples, and cordially waving to one another.

The Whipple milkman emerged from an antique shop, his cap pulled low over his face. He held an old wooden case on his shoulder. No one noticed how the white uniform hung from the man's scrawny frame, nor that he was far less talkative than normal. His kind smile and tips-of-the-hat put everyone at ease. It was the role of Steve's lifetime.

The plan was for Steve to get Whipple's attention on the other side of town. Then he'd duck down an alley, ditch the uniform in a trashcan, and make his way back to the rest of the group. Hopefully, the inexperienced killers, caught up in the thrill of the hunt, would chase the real milkman long enough for them all to escape.

Just a few minutes. That was all they needed.

Two minutes ticked by. Gavin exited the shop next, trying to appear as nonchalant as possible, even though sweat covered his entire body. The outdated clothes he'd put on were from the racks in the antique shop…which, of course, helped him fit in right with the rest of Whipple. The cardigan-wearing pastor waved at him, and Gavin waved back and relaxed. Mars had been right: No one had seen Gavin on Main Street, in the diner, or on the gallows. No one knew he was a carnie too.

He ambled away from the antique store, hands in his pockets, mustering all the acting talent he didn't have. His eyes bounced from vehicle to vehicle, looking for the ideal getaway car to hotwire. He had a wire hanger in his back pocket to help unlock any car he chose.

Marsuvees peeked through the shop's glass door. The moment Steve and Gavin were each out of sight, his heart rate spiked. They were out there in this hellish town, alone. He was their ringmaster, and here he was cowering—

"They'll do great, Mars." Jasmine set a hand on his arm. "Trust them."

The ringmaster pulled his cape around himself and nodded. "You're right, you're right."

All they could do was wait. Wait and trust. Two things Marsuvees the Magnificent had never been great at.

It didn't take long.

A townsperson on the street yelled, "They've spotted the kid! He's by the fountain!"

"What's he doing over there?" another asked.

"He's..." A shrug. "He's doing the '*To be or not to be*' speech."

Mars chuckled and shook his head. That was Steve for sure.

In a matter of seconds, the citizens vacated Main Street, charging across town like a poisonous fog.

Marsuvees counted down from five, then sprung open the shop door. He and Jasmine needed to make it as far to the edge of the town as possible so that Gavin wouldn't have to weave through the streets in the getaway car.

He squinted against the pale sunlight and began to move quickly across the street, but a voice shattered the silence.

"Gotcha!" a too-happy male voice yelled. Mars spun to see Frank—the man who'd operated the old-fashioned camera at their hanging—charging toward them, holding a wrench high above his head. The smile careened forward, and Mars felt like he was about to be flattened by Thomas the Tank Engine.

Marsuvees's body might have been past its prime, but his reflexes were spot-on. In a flash, he pushed Jasmine out of the way and dodged the wrench as Frank brought it down. The Whipplian cocked his arm to hit the ringmaster with a follow-up backswing, but Marsuvees had another idea.

A mischievous grin split his face as he clutched the sides of his cape with both hands. In the moments before Frank swung the wrench,

Marsuvees spun with a grand flourish. The piano wire lining his cape wasn't as sharp as the garrote he preferred back in the day, but his adrenaline made up for it. The speed and velocity sliced deep into Frank's forearm, and he immediately let go of his weapon. It flew through the air and clattered to the asphalt.

The photographer stared at the ringmaster with eyes like golf balls, then retreated as fast as he could. If he had a tail, it would've been tucked firmly between his legs.

Jasmine shot Mars a smile and a nod. "I've been wanting to see that lil maneuver for a while now."

"Frank! Come back, please!"

The two Olympians turned to find Roy the diner-owner wielding an axe. He seemed far more comfortable with his weapon than Frank did with his.

"Fine, I'll do it myself."

Mars quickly estimated that his cape wasn't long enough to slice Roy while staying outside the axe's reach. He and Jazz took off down Main Street, and Roy gave chase. He was as jolly pursuing people with an axe as he was serving eggs.

The diner-owner was quicker on his feet than he looked. He closed the distance and began chopping at his opponents with vigor. Mars and Jasmine barely remained one step ahead, bobbing and weaving down the street.

Mars gripped his cape and swung, aiming for Roy's meaty fingers around the axe's handle, but the Whipplian was faster. He caught the flowing fabric around his blade and yanked upward. Marsuvees could only watch as his cape was sliced in two.

"No!" he cried in shock and anguish. He and that cape had been together for decades, and in a matter of seconds, it was completely destroyed.

Roy breathed heavily and beamed. "It was a pleasure serving you two this morning." Malice dripped from his cordial smile.

He lifted his arms to bury the axe in Marsuvees's head, but one more voice joined the fray.

"Oh hellooooooo..."

A garish falsetto.

Roy froze. He turned. He shrieked.

Behind him stood a bony college kid wearing a milkman's cap. White paint was smeared all over his face, congealing in the cold air and cracking wherever his face moved. Red paint dribbled from his lips and chin like blood.

His eyes were crazed—those of a true freak. And he too had an axe.

"I found youuuuuuu."

Marsuvees and Jasmine seized the opportunity to take cover. But Mars couldn't resist one more glance over his shoulder. Pride smoldered in his gut. He'd never seen Steve so submerged in the character of Zobo the Clown.

In fact, Steve was gone.

"Where are all the friggin' axes coming from?" Jasmine muttered.

Roy swallowed the lump in his throat and took a tentative step toward the hellish figure. "Now you listen here—"

Zobo unhinged his jaw and let loose the most bloodcurdling, maniacal laugh Marsuvees had ever heard in his career full of maniacs.

To Roy's credit, he stood his ground longer than Frank did. A full three seconds longer. As soon as Zobo began sprinting, swinging his axe like a fishing rod, the diner-owner turned to run. But nothing is faster than insanity.

Marsuvees blinked, and the killer clown was on top of the Whipplian, axe buried in his back up to the hilt. Roy jerked once, twice, then never again.

Zobo stood tall and wiped the syrupy red fluid from his face—it wasn't clear if it was paint or blood anymore. He exhaled, like a lion after catching and devouring its prey.

"Knife to meet you." He slapped his forehead. "Oh, it's an axe, not a knife." Steve was back, squeaky voice and all. "I-I-I'm so sorry, Mr. Magnificent, I really fudged it up."

"It's alright, my boy, quite alright!" Marsuvees cautiously approached the college kid and patted his shoulder. Somehow, his entire impression of Steve had radically changed in the last sixty seconds. Now, there was a lightswitch in the middle of his forehead that could release a ravenous beast at any moment.

And Mars loved it.

Tires screeched against asphalt, and a big gray van peeled onto Main Street. Marsuvees saw Gavin hunched over the wheel, vibrating in his seat.

They were so close to escape.

Gavin brought the van to a screeching halt beside his three friends. "Get in, get in, get in!"

Almost home free.

BOOM.

Buckshot peppered the hood of the van, letting black smoke escape with a *hiss.*

"Get out of the van!" Rhonda, the mayor of Whipple, marched into the middle of Main Street, a monstrous twelve-gauge pump-action shotgun in his grip. Her smile twitched, and it looked like her teeth were about to shatter from the pressure of her jaws. "*Now.*"

Gavin raised his hands in surrender and tumbled out of the driver's seat, the van's engine sputtering but still kicking. He took his place amongst the other Olympians, who also inched their hands above their shoulders.

Mars, estimating that about ten feet separated them, looked Rhonda in the eye. "Now, Madam Mayor, blasting us away won't earn you many style points."

"At this point..." She trilled a shaky laugh that quickly replaced Steve's as the most terrifying in history. "Points are points!"

"Rhonda..." Marsuvees stepped forward to bridge the gap, but the mayor would have none of it. She fired again at the street mere inches in front of Mars, and tar shrapnel buried itself in his exposed skin like hot coals. His hands and face sizzled, and he cried out and fell to his knees.

"Mars!" Jasmine shouted and knelt beside him.

"I'm done playing with my food!" Rhonda pumped another shell into place and aimed.

Jasmine the Fortune Mage held Mars's face between her hands. "Hang tight, pal." Then, in a flash, she ripped the silver pocketwatch from his waistcoat. Before Mars could object, she stood and faced Rhonda.

"Missus," Jasmine held up her hands in what looked like surrender and began taking tiny, tiny steps toward the murderous mayor. But the watch dangled from the middle finger of her right hand, casually swinging with her steps.

"I'm warning you!" Rhonda held the shotgun eye-level.

"Just listen for a minute." Jasmine used a soft tone, one that forced Rhonda to strain her ears to listen. "You and I are very similar. We're short on time. Seconds tick by, and we can't stop them. We only want to leave legacies that will be adored for years to come. You're trying to make a legacy, aren't you, Rhonda? You're a proud, strong woman. You built this town all by yourself. It's great because of *you*. But this town let you down. It let your legacy slip right through your fingers. It's not your fault. It's *theirs*."

Rhonda's eyes were glazed over, her smile trembling as if it was bearing too much weight. Her arms went limp, and the shotgun clattered to the ground.

Jasmine prompted, "Whose fault is it?"

"Theirs." Rhonda's voice was clear and strong.

"They let your legacy go."

"They let my legacy go."

Jasmine stopped right in front of the mayor, holding the watch aloft. "Maybe *they* can take the circus's place."

"They can take the circus's place." Rhonda walked with confidence to a car parked next to a meter, unlocked it, and got in. Gaze fixed directly ahead, she fired up the engine and careened into Whipple.

Jasmine smirked back at the three men.

They stared in awe. Marsuvees's heart almost glowed through his chest.

She tossed up the pocketwatch and caught it. "Haven't done that in a few years."

Marsuvees inhaled the crisp air. "Jazz, you're a marvel." He clapped once. "Now, to the van! We can't take any more chances."

The four Olympians piled into the smoking van, Mars in the driver's seat, Jasmine next to him, Gavin and Steve in the back.

"Wh-What did you make her do?" Steve asked. He removed the milkman's cap and began wiping off Zobo.

"Well, hypnotism is all about suggestion, and suggestion kinda blossoms independently. I basically told her to kill Whipple instead of Olympia."

Marsuvees tapped the gas pedal, and the van lurched forward. It had enough life in its engine to get them out.

Screams echoed from the other side of town. A revving engine, skidding wheels, deep thuds, and sickly squishes.

Mars recalled how Rhonda had mentioned she'd killed Whipple's first victims: running them over with her car. Now, it seemed all of Whipple would soon succumb to the same fate.

He rolled down Main Street and took what he dearly hoped was his very last look at the town that had nearly killed him and his friends. He was driving at what was sure to be vastly over the speed limit, but he doubted any Whipple cops would notice. They had another case of road rage to deal with on the opposite side of town.

Just like that, the buildings vanished, and the city proper ended. The van raced down the road, trees whizzing past in a blur.

A figure stood on the left side of the road up ahead, thumb out. As they passed, all four carnies leaned in for a closer look at the hitchhiker.

It was a tall man wearing a black, full-length rain slicker. A black fisherman's hat obscured his face. Black boots swallowed his feet. One hand was extended, thumbing for a ride. The other clutched a rusty hook. He may as well have been holding a sign that said, *"Hello, I'm a serial killer."*

Marsuvees pressed harder on the gas pedal and zoomed right by.

Jasmine let out a thoughtful grunt.

"What is it, Jazz?"

"Huh?" She looked over at the ringmaster, holding onto the drifting notion in her mind. "Eh, I was just thinking. I don't think anyone in the Group Division has taken out a Slasher before. That's gotta be worth good points."

Steve smirked from the backseat. "Imagine the headlines in the next newsletter."

Marsuvees the Magnificent, ringmaster of the Olympia Traveling Circus, checked the time on his pocketwatch. "Well, the rest of the crew has been waiting for us all morning." He whipped the steering wheel around and sped back toward the ominous hitchhiker. "They can wait a bit more."

The van filled with triumphant cheers. Gavin patted the ringmaster's shoulder, and Jasmine's eyes lit up. Mars straightened his waistcoat as he gripped the wheel, electricity running through his veins for the first time in years. Decades.

"What a day."

About the Author:

LUKE SWANSON WAS RAISED on a steady diet of stories. Each of his novels has dabbled in a new genre: murder mystery, fantasy adventure, action thriller, dystopian satire, and cozy mystery...so far. He has also adapted three of his works in screenplays, one of which was a finalist in two online festivals. He lives with his wife in Oklahoma City.

• • • •

"Lovers of Shakespeare will enjoy this romp through the life and times of his characters, which proves beyond a doubt that all the world's a stage."
-Ian Doescher, author of "William Shakespeare's Star Wars"

• • • •

"It's an entertaining and humorous tale that shows off Swanson's razor-sharp wit. Full of adventure, tension, and expert storytelling, this is Swanson at his very best!"
-Kiersten Modglin, author of "I Said Yes" and "The Arrangement"

"Catch-22 for the Black Mirror era. This book, like all good satire, has one foot firmly planted in the real world."
—Nathan Allen, author of "Horrorshow"

• • • •

"Kaleidoscopic, hilarious, and intelligent. The characters are all perfectly realized and will stick with you long after you finish reading. It's a real page-turner with genuine heart."
—Henry Hinder, author of "Bad Strings" and "The Kid Who Shot the Archduke"

"*A love letter to theatre, Christmas, and Agatha Christie all wrapped in one.*"
—*Timothy Gene Sojka, author of* "*Payback Jack*"

• • • •

"*The Muppet Christmas Carol meets Clue. A beautifully wrapped holiday present for theatre kids and cozy mystery lovers alike.*"
—*B.A. McRae, author of* "*The World Ends Christmas Day*" *and* "*I've Never Danced*"

About the Cover Artist:

COLSON WOODARD IS AN artist based in Oklahoma who specializes in character illustrations and silly sketches for kids. When he's not drawing, he spends his time LEGO-building, playing pickleball, and hanging out with his wife Emmie.

www.ingramcontent.com/pod-product-compliance
Lightning Source LLC
Chambersburg PA
CBHW071940170626
46813CB00005B/1800